Much Ado About

GRUBSTAKE

Much Ado About

GRUBSTAKE

JEAN FERRIS

SCHOLASTIC INC.
New York Toronto London Auckland Sydney
Mexico City New Delhi Hong Kong Buenos Aires

ISBN-13: 978-0-545-07135-2
ISBN-10: 0-545-07135-6

12 11 10 9 8 7 6 5 4 3 2 1   8 9 10 11 12 13/0

Printed in the U.S.A.   40

First Scholastic printing, January 2008

Text set in New Century Schoolbook
Designed by Lauren Rille

FOR
PAT LITTELL
WITH THANKS FOR LETTING ME BORROW HER FAMILY

Grubstake, Colorado

APRIL 1888

ONE

SIX ELEPHANTS COULD HAVE gotten off the monthly train and they wouldn't have been as big a deal to Arley as her precious box of Penny Dreadfuls. Making them last until the next train brought more was one of the hardest things she did—and that was saying something, considering how hard she worked every day at her boarding house.

In the Penny Dreadfuls things *happened*. Did they ever! People got kidnapped by pirates, or drunk on champagne, or married to the wrong people, or thrown in jail, or chased by bandits. It was wonderful.

Nothing ever happened in Grubstake. Big fat nothing. Gallons of nothing. Tons of nothing. Miles of nothing. The mines were played out, and the only people left in town were the ones who had no place else to go. The Opera House had shut down when Arley was little. The schoolmarm had married the fellow who mined the last of the silver, and they'd gone off to live in Denver, letting marmots (who were pretty good neighbors, but lousy housekeepers) move into the abandoned schoolhouse. The train had cut its schedule down to once a month, and most of the houses built during the bonanza days were gradually succumbing to time and weather.

Considering all that, Arley should have paid more attention to the stranger getting off the train, since a visitor was such a rare occurrence. She would have, too, if she hadn't been so busy juggling her box of books while trying to pull her dogs, Wilbur and Orville, away from a couple of crates with heavy screens on the front. Restless, growly sounds came from the crates, along with the scratch and click of... could it be claws?

But if Arley wasn't paying attention to the stranger, others were. Her boarders, mainly. Watching the train arrive was their entertainment for the month. They saw the fellow with the snappy plaid suit, the shiny city shoes, and the pomaded blond hair under the derby hat come down the steps. While the man waited for his baggage—rather a lot of it—to be unloaded,

Prairie Martin wheedled from the conductor the facts that the fellow had gotten on in Denver, his luggage was brand new, and he'd flashed a wallet full of greenbacks when he paid for his dining car meal. But the biggest question remained unanswered: What was somebody like him doing in a place like Grubstake?

The conductor had only shrugged. As the train pulled away for the long descent off the mountain, the gossip and speculation began. The stranger was a salesman, selling something that would change their lives. Or he was running from the law, and what better place to hide out than remote, forgotten Grubstake? Or he had a fatal illness and had come there to die so none of his greedy family members would find his suitcases full of money. Or he had lost his memory and was trying to find a place that seemed familiar.

And what about those crates? They seemed to be his, too. Oh, this fellow could keep the Grubs occupied for days as their stories became more bizarre and tangly. Finding out too soon what he was really doing there, especially if it was something as ordinary as a mistake, could spoil all their fun.

Arley would get in on all of that later. For now, she just wanted to get her dogs away from those crates, take her box home, open it, and revel in the smell of new books and the promises hiding behind titles like

Badgirl in the Badlands, The Danger of a Texas Ranger, and *Rustler's Rhapsody.* Every page was heaven for a sixteen-year-old girl who believed with all her heart that her life was over. Oh, she might live to be 98½, but her last day would be indistinguishable from any of the thousands that had come before: chores, tending to her boarders, and watching the high mountain seasons change (short spring, shorter summer, a couple of weeks of fall, and endless winter).

The last exciting thing to happen in Grubstake had been the one that had put her in this predicament. Two years before, Arley's own father, never much good with dynamite, blew himself out of his mine and into Kingdom Come—with a few swell loop-the-loops as he went.

Since her mother had died when she was born, Arley was suddenly on her own in a big way. So by the age of fourteen, she'd already figured out there weren't any happy endings in real life. Or any endings at all, really, except for that final one. Life just kept bumping along, up sometimes, down others, until it didn't anymore. But Penny Dreadfuls always had happy endings, in spite of the dastardly villains, the earthquakes, the shootings, and the betrayals along the way. They were delicious company during the long, long winters.

Arley put the box of books in the little wagon she used for errands and began pulling it home through the muddy streets. In the center of Grubstake, a wooden sidewalk ran alongside the hotel and saloon, Mickey's livery, the newspaper office, the bakery, the pathetic excuse for a restaurant, and the general store. Arley clattered along the wooden slats, glad to be out of the mud for a minute. Once she'd tried hitching Orville and Wilbur to the wagon, but their reputation as the worst-behaved dogs in town held true and they'd run off with it, spilling the contents and knocking Mrs. Bernaise, the doctor's wife, into a puddle.

When Grubstake was a boomtown, there had been restaurants, saloons, and shops, a tailor, a milliner, a blacksmith, and a laundry. But that heyday had been brief—as long as the silver and gold came easily—and then it was over. Those who could do so moved on to richer places. Those who couldn't, stayed—and some of them lived at Arley's.

Everdene Hannigan, the owner of the hotel and saloon, was standing in the doorway of the Spittoon as Arley and the dogs went by. Everdene's mop of red curls was piled artfully on her head; her black-and-blue striped dress was amply filled by her curves. Arley sighed and unconsciously ran one hand down her own slim torso. It was hopeless. She ate like a lumberjack, but something as sumptuous as Everdene apparently grew from more than ordinary food.

"Hey, Lemon Drop," Everdene greeted her. "How you doing this gray morning? Got your books, I see." Everdene had called her Lemon Drop since she was a baby. Lemon drops were Everdene's favorite candy because they were pretty, sweet, and sharp all at the same time.

"Hey, Everdene. I'll pass them on to you as soon as I read them."

"Not the romancey ones. Just the blood-and-thunder ones."

"Some of the romantic ones are good."

"Not a subject that interests me. No way. Not in the slightest. But blood and thunder, that's good. Say, I hear some city slicker got off the train just now."

"I think so. I couldn't pay much attention. There were these crates that got unloaded from the train. They had something in them that made the dogs go nuts. But you ought to be seeing the stranger pretty soon. After all, it's not as though there are a bunch of hotels in town."

Everdene hugged herself and shivered. "I sure wish it would warm up. Doesn't it seem like this winter's gone on forever? I want to put my swinging doors up on the Spittoon. A saloon needs swinging doors. But I can't until it gets warm."

"I'm pretty sick of all the rain myself. Makes it hard to get my boarders' laundry done."

Everdene peered down the street toward the station. "That must be him coming, the guy from the train. It's been so long since we had a guest here, I'm not sure I can remember how it works."

"You will," Arley said, moving on. "You always know what to do. See you later."

Arley used to wish her father would marry Everdene and then Everdene would be her real mother instead of just the person who took care of her at the Spittoon every day while her father was at the Never Mine. But Everdene was opposed to men, at least in a romantic way. She said she'd been burned by love early and knew all she cared to know about it forever. Arley was pea-green with envy at the drama suggested by that statement, but Everdene never would say any more. Every miner in Grubstake was in some degree of love with her, but she wasn't interested. Considering the selection, Arley couldn't be surprised.

Arley passed the newspaper office, hurrying to keep up with the dogs, who always went faster when they got close to home and food. She looked in through the glass front window at Duncan McKenzie, the editor of *The Expositor*. He knew all the big words in the dictionary, and used them every day. He was only three years older than Arley, yet she thought he seemed much more grown-up. Maybe because he was so tall and handsome, so smart and serious. Sort of like Jesse, the hero in *Gunfire on the Pecos*. But Jesse fell for the doctor's daughter, something Arley was afraid Duncan was going to do, too.

Arley waved but he didn't see her. As usual. She sighed a big bunch of sighs and slogged on home.

When she opened the back door, juggling her box of books, the dogs flung themselves past her, leaving a trail of mud into the kitchen, where all the best indoor things seemed to happen. After sniffing the air for cooking smells—no, nothing there—they snuffled around for any of the boarders, who were usually pungent enough to find in the dark. Nothing there, either. They flopped themselves under the kitchen table, where there was always hope of falling scraps, and settled down to wait.

Well, they'll just have to wait a little longer, Arley thought, flinging off her bonnet and popping the twine around her box with a yank powered by arms strong from chopping firewood, hauling wet wash, and dragging the occasional mule out of her garden. She couldn't wait to see what was inside.

The twenty beautiful new Penny Dreadfuls had to last a month until the next train came. Maybe if she read them each twice, they would. The covers were rich with gaudy colors, lurid scenes, and enticing fragments: "...she knew it was wrong, but she was helpless in his arms...," "...at that moment, he knew they would meet again, probably in violent circumstances...," "...the moon went behind a cloud as he took out his stiletto...." She shivered with anticipation.

But first, supper. She carried the box upstairs to her bedroom and then hit the kitchen to start cooking. Beans again, this time with wild onions and one of the last jars of the tomatoes she'd canned last summer. Considering the infrequency with which her boarders paid their rent, stretching the budget had become her most challenging task.

—◦◦◦◦◦◦—

Around the supper table, the stranger from the train was the only topic of conversation. Now Arley was wishing she'd paid more attention to him. There was agreement that he sure didn't look like a miner, that he wasn't anybody's relative (when a town has only sixty-two residents, that's a question that can be answered pretty fast), and that nobody had known he was coming. The table full of old miners had been handed enough tantalizing mystery to chew on for months—and there must be more to come. They felt like they'd struck a rich vein for the first time in years.

As exasperated as the old guys could make her, Arley was happy to see them so lively. There had been many dinners eaten in silence after yet another day of fruitless prospecting, and even the dogs hated that. Gloomy diners forgot to offer them bites.

"Did you see those crates?" Purvis asked for the sixth time.

Purvis needed things explained to him over and over—and even then Arley wasn't quite sure he got it. In fact, he'd arrived in Grubstake by accident years before when he'd been unable to understand a railroad schedule and boarded the wrong train. He'd meant to go to St. Louis.

"Something in there was alive, I'm sure of it," he went on.

"Nobody's disagreeing with you," Zeb said, a little impatiently. Zeb was always a little impatient, which is probably why, though he bragged about having once made a living as a cardsharp, every time he shuffled the cards, he went too fast and they flew all over the place. "For the sixth time, we all heard it."

"Well, what do *you* think it is?" Purvis asked.

"You think I know and I just won't tell you?" Zeb asked testily. "Nobody knows. Don't you get it?" He stood, his plate of dried-apple pie in his hand, turned, and left the dining room. They heard his footsteps going upstairs.

Purvis's lower lip trembled. "Did I say something wrong?"

Arley jumped up with the coffeepot, putting her hand on his shoulder as she poured him more. "He's just in a bad mood. As usual. He's...you know...disappointed."

"He's not the only one," Outdoor John said. "And *we* don't act like that. We could, but we don't."

It wasn't bad enough that the leftover miners were disappointed—they also felt unworthy. That was because of the old Indian legend that had come with the town and with the mines. The spirits of the Utes who had originally lived on the land now claimed by Grubstake were supposedly still there, watching over their old hunting grounds. And being pretty crabby about it, too.

The legend said they allowed only the most deserving and pure of heart to benefit from the richness of the mountains, and that they would punish those who weren't worthy. From what Arley had seen, they weren't very discriminating. Her boarders, though they definitely had their quirks, seemed a lot more deserving to Arley than some of the yo-yos, boneheads, and outlaws who struck it rich and hotfooted it down the mountain to spend their treasure as fast as they could. Or maybe that was the punishment—to leave the beauty of the mountains and the companionship of the other Grubs, and go down to some crowded city where they could go broke in a hurry. Arley's boarders didn't see it that way. They felt punished by the paltriness of their strikes, yet were committed to staying in Grubstake since none of them had any other place to go. And they wondered if that was part of their punishment, too.

Arley believed in the spirits. She knew some of the Grubs thought she read too many Penny Dreadfuls, that the curious and dramatic things that happened in the books made her believe that they could happen in real life, too. But she believed she had felt those old spirits sometimes, lingering beside her, admiring the view, when she stood behind her house and looked up to the mountains where snow stayed on the very tops year round. When the wind sang through the pines scattered up the steep hillsides, she thought she could hear whispers in a language she didn't understand.

She didn't know why the spirits were as capricious as they seemed to be, but she figured that was their business—and maybe they even knew what they were doing, whether she understood it or not.

Arley watched Outdoor John stroking Wilbur's

head, which was resting hopefully on the old miner's lap. He seemed to be professionally feeling all the bumps and dents in Wilbur's skull. Outdoor John's hobby was taxidermy and, though he was too soft-hearted (and also too afraid of guns) to outright kill any specimens, he wasn't averse to bringing home the already dead things he found in the mountains. Arley had to brace herself pretty hard before she went in to clean his room, and always rewarded herself afterwards with a couple of chapters of *Clarissa and the Cowboy.*

Arley sat again and told Purvis, "Just imagine Zeb going down the mountain on a runaway mule," she said. "Or locked out of the house in his underwear in the rain. That's what I do when anybody makes me mad. And then I always feel better."

"You ever think that about me?" Purvis asked, with more trembling.

"I never get mad at you, Purvis," she said almost truthfully. It was pretty hard—though not impossible—to get mad at somebody like Purvis, who spent hours carefully writing out sayings (dreadfully misspelled ones, to be sure) on parchment, and then painstakingly decorating the page with illustrations in colored ink and gold leaf. Arley's favorite was Thanx for the good cooken, washen, and havin a haus *fer us.* It's true his room was a mess of paper scraps and spilled ink, but that was definitely better than the three-day-old weasel carcasses that turned up in Outdoor John's room.

Purvis smiled shyly down at his plate.

"What about me?" Prairie Martin asked, his cheeks pinking above his beard. "Do you see me in my...you know...out in the rain?"

"I see your you-knows a lot more often in the laundry," Arley said. Everything he wore had little blots of wax on it since he liked to whittle gnomes out of candle stubs. That made his room a serious fire hazard. One of the reasons Arley liked to imagine him out in the rain was because that way it would be hard for him to start a fire.

"And me?" Outdoor John asked.

What she wanted to say was *Oh, come on, you guys, grow up.* But she wasn't sure anybody ever really did—especially orphans, which they all were. So instead, she said, "Not you, either."

Mostly it was Lacey Bernaise, the doctor's daughter, that she imagined on the mule or in the rain, but she wasn't going to tell them that.

Satisfied, the miners dug in to their pie.

With his mouth full, Prairie Martin said, "So do you think there'll be more in the *Expositor* this week than what Orville and Wilbur have been up to, or more of that story Duncan's working on?"

Prairie Martin couldn't make up his own mind about anything, and was forever asking Arley what her opinion was, forcing her to have one even when she really didn't. In fact, he'd arrived in Grubstake as the result of getting on the first train that pulled into his station since he couldn't decide which one he really *wanted* to take.

"I think our stranger will definitely be news," she said. "And there'll also be Duncan's story *and* news about the dogs. You can count on it."

Because there was so little news in Grubstake, Duncan had taken to writing serialized stories to fill up space in the paper. They were all about down-on-their-luck miners who unexpectedly hit a mother lode of gold or silver, copper or lead. The Grubs loved them and could hardly wait for the next installment.

⁕

While Arley cleaned up the kitchen, Prairie Martin sat at the table and serenaded her with his harmonica. Everybody said (at least to his face) that he was a brilliant player, but Arley, who had never heard anybody else play the harmonica, thought that if Prairie Martin was brilliant, she sure didn't want to hear anybody who was bad. And the worst of it was that the dogs were big fans and liked to sing along until Arley was practically deaf. It was a big relief when he finished his concert and went up to bed.

Once the dishes were put away, she opened the back door to let the dogs out for one last run before bed. They couldn't stay out long because there was a full moon, even if it wasn't entirely visible because of the rain clouds. On full moon nights they could incite every other dog in town to bay along with them for hours, until they were all hoarse and coughing and bruised from the shoes and kitchen utensils thrown at them to shut them up.

Arley glanced down at the doorstep and noticed a flyer lying there.

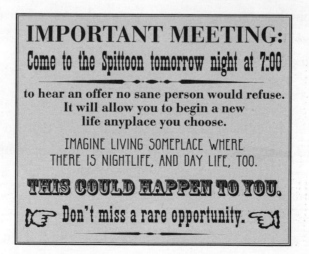

IMPORTANT MEETING:
Come to the Spittoon tomorrow night at 7:00

to hear an offer no sane person would refuse.
It will allow you to begin a new
life anyplace you choose.

IMAGINE LIVING SOMEPLACE WHERE
THERE IS NIGHTLIFE, AND DAY LIFE, TOO.

THIS COULD HAPPEN TO YOU.

Don't miss a rare opportunity.

Well, she didn't have to be a genius to know the important meeting had something to do with the city slicker from the train. One thing she would bet big money on—if she had any—was that all sixty-two Grubs would be at the Spittoon at 7:00 the next night.

Two

AT BREAKFAST, AFTER SHE'D put the platters on the table and the miners had instantly scooped the contents onto their plates and begun scarfing them down, Arley waved the flyer.

"Take a look at this," she said.

They all stopped chewing and looked up.

She read the flyer (three times, at Purvis's request) and then had to pass it around from one greasy hand to the next.

"So what's it mean?" Purvis asked.

"I don't know," Arley said. "That's why I'll be going to the meeting. And I expect you will be, too."

"Do you think I should go?" Prairie Martin asked.

"Yes," she said, making up his mind for him. "Definitely."

"All *right,*" he said, beaming. "I'm going to the meeting."

Zeb, Outdoor John, and Purvis had been muttering among themselves while Arley and Prairie Martin talked. Then Zeb spoke up. "You think this has anything to do with that fellow who came on the train yesterday?"

Honestly, Arley thought, *these guys spend way too much time underground.* "Well," she said, "since nobody new has come to Grubstake for a long time, and since we don't know anybody else in town who might offer us a new life, that would sure be my guess."

"Do you think he's dangerous?" Outdoor John asked. He was afraid of almost everything. He'd come to Grubstake with an acquaintance—who later left—because he was afraid to go anywhere alone. The only thing he wasn't afraid of was going down in a mine, which was the thing that scared Arley the most. Even though she was now the owner of the Never Mine, she had never been farther into it than the adit, the mine's entrance.

"No," she said, being decisive for Prairie Martin and reassuring for Outdoor John at the same time. "And don't ask me why," she said, heading off Purvis's need for an explanation. "It's just my instincts." She wasn't even sure she had any instincts, but it was an answer nobody could argue with. Mostly, she didn't want Outdoor John worrying himself sick with fear if he didn't have to. They could all worry later, if necessary.

"What do you think about him?" Prairie Martin asked.

She willed herself not to roll her eyes. They'd worried this subject over and over at dinner last night like Orville and Wilbur sharing a meaty bone. Except that the dogs weren't so good at sharing.

"I already told you I didn't pay much attention when he got off the train. But we've heard he's a sharp dresser—who else around here wears a plaid suit? And he's from the big city and he has a pocketful of money. That's all any of us knows about him right now. I think we should hear what he has to say before we finish deciding what to think about him." That sounded good to her. Reasonable and moderate and sensible. But apparently she did have some instincts because something in her head was more than just curious. It was suspicious.

"You think it's true we could begin a new life anywhere we choose?" Zeb asked. "You think that's possible?"

Zeb had been the first one in Grubstake to dig up

a few big gold nuggets, so he'd thought the Indian spirits liked him and that he was on his way to Easy Street. Then he never again found anything more than bits of gold dust, and had felt undeserving and glum about it ever since. More than the others, for some reason, in spite of their having had similar experiences. Maybe they were more resilient. Or tougher. Or just too dim to really understand their situation.

"Yes," Arley said firmly, because it happened all the time in Penny Dreadfuls, even though she'd seen no signs of it in her real life. But Zeb needed to think so. Probably they all did. "Definitely."

"You think there's money involved?" Outdoor John asked. He was always anxious about money, afraid he wouldn't have enough to buy the supplies he needed for stuffing and mounting his specimens. The monthly train was important to him, too, because it brought the taxidermy gear he waited for as impatiently as Arley did her books. This month he had received a box of Fur Fluffer and a precious jar of Rodent Repair that had been on back order for months.

"I don't doubt it," Arley said. "That would be the only thing he could offer everybody that they couldn't refuse, is what I think."

"You think we should take it?" Prairie Martin asked. Wilbur and Orville each had his chin resting on one of Prairie Martin's knees and, while they may only have been waiting for a chance to snatch a sausage from his fingers, Arley knew Prairie Martin liked to believe that they enjoyed his company.

"I think we should wait. We don't know for sure there's money involved," Arley said. "We don't really know *anything*. So I'd advise you all to finish your breakfasts, go to your mines, come home and have supper, and then we'll go to the meeting and see what's what."

She sat down to her own sausages and eggs and wondered how people who needed as much help with dailiness as these guys did could ever start new lives in places of their own choosing. How would they ever be able to *make* a choice?

As soon as the boarders had left, Arley cleaned up the kitchen, split some firewood, built a fire in the backyard, hung the wash kettle over it, filled the kettle with multiple bucketsful from the well, and gathered up the miners' dirty laundry (she wore her toughest gardening gloves for this task—and sometimes still had to use tongs). She yanked her bonnet on over her unruly curls and headed off to the *Expositor* office while she waited for the water to boil. She needed to have a talk with Duncan, even if he was so handsome and so, so . . . well, so totally perfect that she usually had a hard time producing coherent speech in his presence. She knew she must seem like a witless ninny to him, but there didn't seem to be anything she could do about it except overcompensate, which then made her sound like a graceless shrew.

It seemed to her that they had something rare in common—losing their fathers in odd circumstances—that should make them unusually compatible, but it didn't seem to be working that way.

Two years before, just after Arley's father blew himself up, Sebastian McKenzie disappeared in a howling blizzard. He was writing an article for the *Expositor* on how the heavy snow that Grubstake got each winter affected the lives of the Grubs. He had set out in his big bearskin coat, the bearskin hat that came down over his eyebrows, and his bearskin mittens and boots to see how long it would take to walk to the Spittoon. There were those who thought his infatuation with Everdene had something to do with his eagerness to get there, even in a vicious snowstorm. But he never made it to the Spittoon, and no one ever saw him again. Duncan was left on his own at seventeen to run the *Expositor,* and to make his decisions without his father's help or criticism.

Arley could have told him, if he'd ever asked, that being left all alone, even by somebody who you sometimes wished *would* just go away and leave you be, wasn't as much of a pleasure as you'd thought it would be.

Duncan's world of journalism was clean and pure and idealistic and important, and her world was— well, everything the opposite. But once in a while a conversation with him was necessary, even if she had to run home and berate herself for her behavior and then look up in the dictionary half the words he used. She braced her shoulders and took a deep breath.

Through the window she could see Duncan bent over the printing press, his sleeves rolled up, his hands covered with ink, his lips moving, probably with cajoling words to the machine.

She pushed open the door and, just as the little bell tinkled, she heard Duncan say a word that wasn't a bit cajoling—and probably wasn't in the dictionary either.

He jerked upright. "Oh. It's you," he said when he spotted Arley. "Did you hear that? Sorry."

Her throat seemed clogged shut. "Uh," she said.

He wiped his hands on a rag and said, "This infernal machine has once again ceased to function correctly and, since this month's train has already departed, I shall either have to devise a remedy or suspend publication until the appropriate components can arrive on a subsequent train."

"Oh," she said. "Yes. Well, I'm sure..." and she petered out. She *knew* he could fix it, and she wanted to tell him so, but nothing more would come out of her mouth.

He stood looking at her in a way she couldn't decipher. Was he thinking how stupid she was? Or was he wishing he could take her in his arms and tell her of his longing for her, the way Clarissa's cowboy did? Not hardly likely. He was probably just wondering what the heck she was doing there if she didn't have any intention of saying anything.

Finally he spoke. "So whose feline have Orville and Wilbur once again chased up a tree? Whose vegetable garden have they yet again excavated? Whose laundry line have they newly demolished, sending the clean garments into the mud?"

She blinked at him.

"Isn't that the rationale for your appearance? Tidings about one or the other of them?"

"Oh. No." Of course. All she meant to him was a news source. Somehow that knowledge loosened her throat. "Well, actually they have done all those things. But what I wanted to know...or to tell you...or to find out if you..." Oh, she was hopeless again. Lacey

Bernaise would never be going on like this. She took the flyer from her pocket. "Did you print this?"

She figured he must have—nobody else in town *could* have—unless the city slicker had brought them with him, which seemed unlikely. He wouldn't have known where the meeting could be held, or when was a good time. "Yes," he said. "That is my handiwork."

"What does it mean?" Oh, why couldn't she make ladylike sounds come out of her mouth when she talked to him? Why did she always sound like either a simpering nitwit or some hard-bitten mule driver? Either too skittish or not enough.

"Well, it means there's to be a meeting at the—"

"I can read," she snapped, and then wanted to put her hand over her mouth. She took a deep breath. "Sorry. What's the meeting *for* is what I want to know. And who's calling it?"

"Oh. Well, that fellow who arrived on yesterday's train bade me prepare the flyer. Charles Randall, he's called. And I have no notion what its purpose is."

"Didn't you *ask*?" She didn't intend to sound so stern but, *really*. If you printed a flyer about an offer no sane person could refuse, wouldn't you just *have* to know what it was?

"Yes. I did inquire. But he declined to enlighten me."

She wanted to kick herself in her own pants. Of

course he would ask! That was his business. He was a *reporter,* for heaven's sake. How could she even have questioned him? "Oh" was all she was able to say.

"He hypothesized that attendance would be greater if the residents' inquisitiveness remained unslaked. I surmise he is correct in that assumption."

She knew the stranger was right about *her* inquisitiveness. If "unslaked" meant unsatisfied. "Are you going?"

"Naturally. News in Grubstake is not abundant—exempting Wilbur and Orville, of course—and I *do* have a newspaper to provide copy for. While I know Grubstake's miners never tire of the stories I've taken to filling the empty pages with, the last thing a journalist wishes to hear is 'another one just like that last one.' It is truly a newspaperman's nightmare—the same item over and over, nothing ever new."

Arley hadn't thought about that before, but she instantly recognized the truth of it. Poor Duncan! Everybody in town knew how critical his father had been of him and his newsmanship. Arley had even heard Sebastian call Duncan a "blot on the family escutcheon." If he hadn't said that, Arley would never have known about that word, not that she ever had any occasion to use it. But Sebastian was wrong. Duncan was good at what he did, and noble. Not too chicken-hearted to aim higher or too mediocre to get there, the way his father kept saying. Maybe the old guy was just trying to be motivating, but if he was, Arley could think of a lot better ways, ones that didn't require the words "chicken-hearted," "mediocre," and "blot," not to mention "escutcheon."

The bell tinkled again and the door opened on Lacey Bernaise, the epitome of femininity in Grubstake (which normally wouldn't have been saying all that much, except that in Lacey's case it was). She flounced in, pointedly ignoring Arley, with her petticoats and parasol and dimity, or whatever that stuff was her mother made her dresses out of.

Her laugh tinkled like the bell on the door when she saw Duncan's smudged face. She put her little lace-gloved hand on his arm and smiled up at him. "I do hope you're going to wash your face before you come over for luncheon."

"My face?"

"You're all inky, you silly boy."

He looked down at his hands. "Oh. I was working...." He gestured toward the printing press.

What good did it do to talk to Lacey about work, Arley wondered sourly, *when she never did any herself?*

Lacey batted her eyelashes at Duncan until she

just couldn't ignore Arley any longer. Her eyelashes came to a halt. "Oh. Hello, Arley."

Arley had learned all about manners from *The Showgirl and the Gentleman,* and had passed the knowledge along (admittedly with little success) to her boarders. The Gentleman would definitely have been disappointed in the Showgirl if she'd cut somebody dead the way Arley wanted to do to Lacey, so she gritted her teeth and said, "Hello, Lacey."

"So what have Wilbur and Orville done now?"

Are those dogs the only interesting things about me? Arley fumed. "Let's see. They cooked dinner last night. They wrote some poetry. And they learned to fly." *What do you make of that, Miss Petticoats?*

"What?" Lacey dropped her gloves.

"I've got to go now," Arley said. She'd had enough of both Lacey and Duncan. Besides, her wash water was probably hot.

"Oh. Good-bye, then," Duncan said, bending to retrieve Lacey's gloves.

Good-bye, then, Arley mimicked to herself as she shut the door. No "Nice of you to stop by." No "I'll see you tonight." No "You're the girl of my dreams." Talk about your bad manners.

THREE

SUPPER THAT NIGHT WAS an agitated affair. None of the boarders—nor Arley either—was used to any kind of excitement and they were out of practice at how to handle it.

"I can't swallow," Outdoor John told Arley. "I think something serious is wrong. I think I should go see Doc Bernaise. Or maybe Wing."

Wing Lee, who ran the town's bakery, also dispensed Chinese medicinal herbs. Ever since he had cured Ed Peavy of the fever and the flux after Dr. Bernaise's treatments had just made him feel worse, Wing's mixtures had become quite popular with the other miners. Arley, too, preferred Wing's odd teas, powders, and potions to Dr. Bernaise's sharp instruments, bitter elixirs, and imperious bedside manner.

"I think you're just overexcited," Arley said. "Take some deep breaths and then drink some water."

He did and gave her a big smile. "You probably saved my life," he said.

"The alignment of the stars is conflicted for tonight," Zeb said. "I've been plotting it out."

Zeb's room was full of star charts and mail-order books about astrology. His aim was to discover when his fortunes would look up, but the heavens seemed to have turned their backs on him just like the Indian spirits had.

"How can you tell?" Arley asked. "It's been cloudy."

"Oh." He waved his left hand carelessly as he spooned up soup with his right. "I know how to do these things. I'm not holding out much hope for anything really life-changing tonight."

Arley never seriously contemplated kicking out any of her boarders, not even the ones who hadn't paid their whole rent for a long time (which was all of them), but if one of them ever *did* leave, she'd vowed to herself that his replacement would be a vivacious optimist.

By 6:45 that evening, the Spittoon held almost every Grub in town. Arley wasn't surprised that Lacey and her mother weren't there, though Dr. Bernaise was. The Bernaise ladies considered themselves too refined to set foot in the place where Arley had been hanging out since she was only a few days old. Dr. Bernaise managed to come in almost every evening for a nip while he was supposed to be walking their tiny, feisty, over-groomed little dog, Fifi. Fifi was too finicky to roll in the mud and duke it out in the alleys over a ripe elk-steak bone like the other dogs of Grubstake. In fact, Arley believed they didn't even consider her a real dog. Occasionally Dr. Bernaise was on hand at the Spittoon during a bar fight and was able to offer immediate medical attention, which normally included ordering a drink for both himself and the injured parties.

Behind the bar Everdene was doing a big business as everyone waited for the meeting to begin. Bridget, the waitress and hotel maid, was distributing liquid refreshments around the room. Arley was glad to see it. Not that she supported public drunkenness, but business had been poor for Everdene since the town had shrunk so much. And Arley didn't know what she'd do if Everdene ever got discouraged enough to leave Grubstake. Or Bridget either. The three of them got together almost every afternoon for a sarsaparilla and a chat, even when there wasn't much to chat about. Everdene might be tough enough to lift a keg of beer over her head, break up a fight between belligerent drunks, and outdraw every man in town, but she'd also had a soft spot for a motherless baby just when that baby needed it the most. And the baby would never forget it.

Maybe a saloon wasn't the finest place for a child to be growing up, what with all the bad language, the occasional gunplay, and the giant portrait of an almost-naked woman on horseback over the bar, but Arley hadn't known that. Hanging out behind the Spittoon's bar with Everdene had been all the fun she'd wanted, and she thought the picture over the bar was absolutely beautiful because it looked so much like Everdene. Sometimes Everdene had refused to serve a regular customer if he got too rowdy around Arley, and Arley would always remember that Everdene had chosen her welfare over hard cash on the barrelhead.

Because the marmots were inhabiting the schoolhouse by the time Arley was of an age to go, Everdene had been her only instructor, even teaching her to read from her own collection of Penny Dreadfuls (just the blood-and-thunder kind) kept on neat shelves in her quarters behind the Spittoon.

Zeb, Purvis, Outdoor John, and Prairie Martin were lined up at the bar, and Arley shook her head as she watched them lay down the meager gold dust that should have been going to pay for their room and board. Oh, well. Maybe tomorrow the big strike would come. She knew it was important to maintain hope, even when things were looking darn hopeless. She also knew it was easier to say that than to do it....

Just as the grandfather clock on the landing of the staircase struck seven, the stranger Duncan said called himself Charles Randall, splendid in a black-and-white houndstooth check suit and his shiny city shoes, came down the steps, casually tucking a watch on a chain into his vest pocket. The room hushed instantly except for Purvis, who could be heard saying, "What does it mean, an offer no *sane* person could refuse?" Then even he stopped talking.

"Ah," Charles Randall said, standing on the landing looking down on them. In more ways than one, Arley had the suspicion. "How nice to see you all tonight. Thank you for coming." He descended the rest of the way down the stairs. Miners swiveled around to keep watching him. He strode to the bar and leaned back, resting his elbows on it. The miners stacked up there backed away until they found places at the tables or against the walls. Something about the man seemed to demand space around him—and not because he smelled bad or was heavily armed as was the usual case in Grubstake.

His blond hair was pomaded precisely into place, his nails manicured, his expression confident, his bearing self-assured. Suddenly Arley, and she suspected everybody else in the room, felt shabby and uncouth and ignorant. She sat up straighter and tucked her work-roughened hands into her skirt pockets. "Let's hear what you've got to say, you big fat city slicker," she muttered.

"This is my first visit to Grubstake," he said—as if they, who scrutinized every movement that happened in their town, wouldn't have known that. "And I'm finding it as charming as I expected to."

The miners looked at each other. Grubstake? Charming?

"So it's no surprise to me that my employer is so interested in the possibility of making a mountain resort of it."

Mountain resort? What kind of resort had a train that came only once a month, a main street that was at the moment a swamp of mud up to one's ankles, and architecture that could most kindly be described as ramshackle? True, the mountain scenery was awe-inspiring—it sometimes brought tears to Arley's eyes—but surely there must be a more congenial place from which to view it.

"He's a magnanimous man and he's authorized me to make each one of you a generous offer for your properties. He's eager to get started on the...uh... improvements."

That would mean every inch of Grubstake, Arley thought.

Purvis spoke up. "What do you mean by generous?"

A rumble of miners' voices followed this question.

"Well, it's a complicated formula since each of you owns a different amount of property. I'd have to speak to you individually. But my starting offer is—" and he named a figure that caused the whole room to catch its breath. They were used to dealing with much smaller numbers. Sometimes ones with minus signs in front of them.

"That would be for the smallest property. One comparable to the mine owned by, say, Zeb Hardy."

Another intake of breath and every face turned to Zeb, who looked as if he'd been hit smartly on the head with a hammer.

"You know my mine?" he managed.

"I know everybody's mine," Charles Randall said placidly.

"You'd pay that much for my mine?" Zeb asked, astonished.

Arley could see where this was going, and she wanted to leap out of her chair and put her hand over Zeb's mouth. Everdene had taught her to play cards, and her first rule of play was to keep a poker face while you collected information. If Zeb had been playing poker, anybody would have known he was holding a royal flush. And there was a lot more he needed to find out before he did what she was afraid he was going to do. Like, what did anybody's mine have to do with a mountain resort? Why couldn't there be a resort *and* mines? She could see Charles Randall wanting to buy the hotel, say, or the long boarded-up Opera House for the resort, but mines? What was up with that?

She stood. Heads swiveled in her direction. They knew her and her big mouth. Well, somebody had to ask the hard questions. "Why would you want to buy Zeb's mine?" she asked.

Charles Randall looked at her. "Ah. Miss Arley Pickett."

She blinked. How did he know her name?

"Miss Arley," he said again, "I wouldn't want to buy it if he didn't want to sell it. I'm here simply at my employer's request, to help you turn your little piece of Paradise into a place many others can enjoy, too."

"But—," she began, before she was drowned out by a bunch of miners all wanting to know what he would offer for *their* properties.

They plainly didn't want her popping their beautiful, unexpected bubble. By then they were so excited and rowdy she couldn't get her voice in to remind them that Charles Randall hadn't answered her question.

Now he was surrounded by miners, all clamoring for his attention. He had moved from the bar to the biggest table, the one where the most cutthroat card games normally took place, and from somewhere he had produced a pad of paper and an account book. He was figuring furiously and Arley could see there was no chance of asking him anything more tonight except "How much?"

She sat down with a discouraged plop and found Wing Lee in the chair beside her, where he hadn't been when she'd stood up.

"Something fishy here," he said. He never said very many words at one time. That usually made people listen. Somehow it was easier to ignore a lot of words than a few.

"Yeah," Arley said.

"Why mines?" Wing Lee asked.

"My question exactly. Which, you might have noticed, he never answered."

"I noticed."

When Arley was a little girl, Wing had come to Grubstake with his two brothers. They'd worked on the railroad and then had done some mining, enough to get themselves started in their own bakery business, which was sufficiently profitable to pay for the other two to return to China. Why Wing stayed on was a mystery to Arley. She guessed Wing saw potential where others, even his brothers, didn't. And Everdene reminded her that since everybody in Grubstake had come from someplace else, too, Wing felt right at home.

Just as she was about to pursue the subject of the resort with Wing, Zeb emerged from the throng and rushed over waving a bill of sale. "Lookie here, Arley. The stars were just being indirect. They do that sometimes. I sold that worthless pit. It's been nothing for years but endless work with no pay dirt. I would have paid *him* to take it off my hands—if I'd had anything to pay him with."

"He gave you cash?" Arley asked. "Right now?"

Zeb pulled a wad of bank notes from his pocket. "Right now," he affirmed. "I'll be out of this place as soon as I can get packed up."

"Where you going?" Wing asked.

Zeb opened his mouth to speak, then closed it and frowned. "Why," he said, "I haven't thought about that. Just out of here was all. And that was enough."

"Got to go somewhere," Wing reminded him.

Zeb stuffed the money back into his pocket. "I will," he insisted. "I'm saddling up Billy and heading down this mountain first thing in the morning. I'll stop when I find a place I like. But I got money now and I can take my time."

"And your chances," Wing told him.

Zeb scowled at him.

"Why don't you stay around a while?" Arley asked. "Figure out what you want to do before you go rushing off somewhere."

She knew how unequipped her miners were for anything but mining. And they didn't do even that very well. Hadn't she been taking care of them for the past two years? Didn't she know all the things about everyday life they had trouble managing? Purvis was helpless when a button came off. When he'd first come to her he was held together completely with safety pins. Outdoor John, for all his familiarity with animal carcasses, couldn't cook anything, not even water (admittedly tricky at 10,000 feet), and was as gaunt as a character in *The Desperate Winter* until she'd fattened him up. Prairie Martin hadn't bathed in months be-cause the creeks were frozen. Arley had to drag him to the bath house Everdene ran on the side of the Spit-toon and where she panned the water for gold dust after each miner finished bathing. And now he had his own back brush, loofah, and bath gel. And Zeb. He was the worst of them all: dirty, ragged, and disorganized in every way—and she'd only just started seeing im-provement after two years of heavy toil on her part. He was totally unprepared for life outside Grubstake. She had to admit, though, that he was looking the hap-piest she'd ever seen him.

"I'm leaving," Zeb insisted. "Don't be trying to talk me out of it. It's all I've thought about for the longest time."

Well, she understood that. Leaving was something *she* thought about, too, even though she knew she hadn't a snowball's chance in, well, in the opposite of Paradise, of it ever happening. In her Penny Dreadfuls she'd read about Paris and San Francisco, New York and London, Denver and Rome—places she knew she'd never see but could imagine in vivid, multicolored de-tail. She'd named the bedrooms in her house after those places, painting the names on the doors. Some-how it made her feel better to think she was going to wash the windows in Paris rather than just in Prairie Martin's room.

Well, she thought. *I tried. If that's how Zeb wants it.* "Then you'd better pay up your back rent before you go." She held out her hand. For once he couldn't use the excuse that he didn't have it.

Carelessly he spilled a few notes into her hand. "That settles it. And then some."

She handed back one note. "That's too much. I only want what's owed me." Sadly, she'd heard of that kind of careless extravagance before, about miners who'd struck it rich and thought there was no end to the money supply. Prudent financial management was a foreign concept to most prospectors. She, on the other hand, could have written a book on the subject with what she'd learned in the years since she became an orphan. Not that any of Grubstake's miners would have bothered to read it.

When she looked up from tucking the bills into her pocket, Wing was gone. How did he *do* that?

She watched Duncan for a while, interviewing the miners who emerged from the clump around Charles Randall with money in their hands. Finally, a story big enough for his talent. But who outside Grubstake would get a chance to see it? *He's the one who should be leaving,* she thought. *Going where his talent could be recognized.* The idea made her heart feel like lead ore in her chest.

She wound her shawl around herself and left, hoping that, by morning, she'd still have some boarders left.

Four

ZEB LEFT THE NEXT MORNING right after breakfast.

Purvis, Prairie Martin, and Outdoor John were still mine-owners because, one, Purvis hadn't understood what was going on, two, Prairie Martin was unable to decide what to do, and, three, Outdoor John was afraid he'd have to leave Grubstake with Zeb, whose company he found too dismal.

Arley packed Zeb a lunch big enough to last for three days and gave him a hug—the first time in two years she'd ever actually touched him. Part of her wished she was going with him—out to the bigger world where adventure awaited. And though she had a mine she would have been thrilled to unload at any price since it was played out *and* she was afraid to set foot in it, she wasn't about to do that until she—along with Purvis—knew what was really going on.

When the other miners had gone off to their mines, she went upstairs to clean Zeb's vacant room. London, it was. He hadn't had much to begin with and he'd taken it all, including every one of his astrology books. There was nothing left to remind her of him except dust bunnies under the bed and a buckle from something— a belt or a saddle or a satchel—on the floor. How exactly like Zeb, to go off with something unbuckled.

Once the room was cleaned, she chopped some firewood, set the beans to soak, and put clean sheets on all the beds—something she'd had to convince her boarders was necessary once in a while. She was sitting at the kitchen table with a cup of tea and *Pamela's Predicament,* which involved a tall man all in black with a scar on his face, when a shadow fell across her teacup. She looked up to see a tall young man, dressed all in black, with a scar slashed across one cheek.

Holy catfish! Were her Penny Dreadfuls coming true? Or was she dozing and dreaming?

Arley jumped up so quickly she spilled her tea as she fumbled in the pocket of her skirt for the little folding knife she always carried. But it was hung up by loose threads. This was the way, she supposed as she struggled to get it loose, that some people lost their lives, their last thoughts having to do with how their final moments were an undignified bungle.

Carrying a knife had always given her the illusion of safety—not that there'd been anything dangerous in Grubstake. Before right now, anyway, when she was realizing how puny a knife was against a stranger in black.

"Who in blazes are you?" Arley demanded, still struggling with her pocket. She had to talk really loud to keep her voice from shaking with fear. And where were Orville and Wilbur, she wondered, when she really needed them? For once they had a chance to do something useful and heroic, and instead they were probably out digging up the petunias she'd been trying to get started in the yard.

"I hear you'll be needing a new boarder," he said in a calm voice that seemed laced with menace.

Arley was actually surprised he wasn't laughing out loud, watching her wrestle with her pocket as if her bloomers were full of ants. His words made her stop. "Who told you that?" she asked in astonishment.

"I heard it at the Spittoon. I wouldn't imagine a vacancy is too easy to fill around here."

She gave up on the knife. She'd just have to fight

him bare-handed if it came to that. But for a moment she was feeling more surprised than scared. "You're looking for a room? Here?"

"I have business," he said in that steely voice. "Business that could take a while."

"Business? In Grubstake?" Arley knew everything about every business in Grubstake, and this guy didn't fit in anywhere. But how did she say no to somebody who looked like he could knock her off without a second thought, and step over her on the way out the door?

"There's business," he said mysteriously.

"What about the hotel?" She cleared her throat to keep her voice from quavering. "They've got rooms over there."

"I don't like the company at the hotel."

He didn't like Everdene? Or Bridget? And then she remembered there was a guest there. "You don't like Charles Randall?"

He gazed at her for a moment and then slapped a handful of gold coins on the table. "Will that do?"

Did he think he could just buy her agreement that easily? She looked at the coins, silently counting them. Did he think she was so easily manipulated?

He added a few more coins to the stack.

That pile would buy enough kerosene for the whole

winter, and flour and sugar and coffee and Penny Dreadfuls and... well, everything.

Was it true, as she'd heard, that everybody had a price?

Apparently so.

"Okay," Arley said weakly. So what if he was dressed all in black, and had a big scar, and could probably break her in two on a whim? So what if she'd sworn her next boarder would be a vivacious optimist? She needed things that gold would buy.

He left the money on the table, then went out and came back in with two bulky saddlebags, which he dumped at the foot of the stairs. "I'm taking Millicent to the livery. I'll be right back." And he left, closing the front door quietly behind him.

She rushed to the window to see him mounting a great big black horse so well brushed that its coat shimmered even in the thin dull mountain light. Millicent? Why, that horse should be named Midnight, or Stormy, or Hellfire. It was then that she realized she knew the horse's name, but not the man's.

Keeping an eye out the window, Arley edged closer to the saddlebags. She kicked one, but it was too heavy to move. Then she sighed, and went back to the kitchen. She wasn't about to commit suicide by getting caught going through the scarred stranger's stuff, no matter how much she wanted to.

Arley was mixing cornbread batter when he returned. "Okay, mister," she said, brandishing her dripping spoon for courage the way she'd wanted to brandish that darn pocket knife. "You need to tell me your name if you're going to be staying here."

He gave her a long level look, and said, "Morgan."

"That's it? Is that your first or your last name? I'm the proprietor of this place, you know. I have to keep records." She'd never kept a record in her life. But it sure sounded official when she said it. And it helped put some starch in her spine.

"Morgan is my name. The only one I have."

"Okay, then, what's your father's name?"

"I never knew him. Or my mother, either. My name is Morgan." He turned and went up the stairs carrying his saddlebags. "What's my room number?" he asked without turning around.

"No numbers. The room that says LONDON on the door."

"London?"

She shrugged, somehow embarrassed in a way she never had been with her usual boarders. "It's just a place that sounded interesting."

"It is," he said as he mounted the stairs.

For a moment Arley forgot to be afraid. "You've been to London? What's it like?"

"Rain. Politics. Theater. Pickpockets. Different from Grubstake."

"No kidding," she muttered. "Except for the rain."

"How do I lock this door?" he called down.

"Oh. There are no locks. I go in to clean. None of my other boarders has anything I shouldn't see." As soon as she said it, she was sorry, as so often seemed to happen with her.

He was standing at the head of the stairs looking down at her with his dark steady gaze. The scar on his cheek seemed more vivid. "How do you know?"

Well, she certainly wasn't going to tell him she knew because she'd looked. "Uh, well, uh, they told me. That's how." She hoped he couldn't see her face clearly from the top of the stairs.

"I carry a set of skeleton keys," he said. "One of them should fit the lock on that door. I'll do my own cleaning."

She heard the keys rattle in the lock until apparently he found one that fit, and then the sound of his door shutting, quietly but firmly.

Who carries skeleton keys, Arley wondered. *Burglars? Police? Other skeletons?*

While the cornbread was baking she could hear Morgan moving around upstairs. Then the sounds stopped, but he didn't come down. She took the cornbread out of the oven and waited, one ear cocked up, but still nothing happened. It was too quiet. Deathly quiet.

She couldn't stay here alone with him.

Arley burst out the door into the chilly and soggy afternoon. And, sure enough, there were her petunias lying uprooted and done for in the yard. Slogging across the muddy street, she realized she'd forgotten her bonnet, something Lacey Bernaise would never do. Lacey would never forget her parasol or her lace gloves, either, or her minuscule reticule that was certainly too small to hold a knife. Oh, well, she wasn't going back across that lake of mud to her house where Morgan was for a bonnet she didn't even need because it wasn't sunny though it wasn't quite raining either. A couple of miners' mules had ambled up and were standing right where she'd have to push them aside to get back to the house anyway. She was thinking she'd better save her energy for whatever Morgan was up to.

She clomped down the wood sidewalk, her boots and the hem of her skirt caked with mud. At Wing's bakery she stood in the doorway and said, "I'm too dirty to come in."

"Out of the mud grows the lotus," he said. "Enter."

Arley did. Wing's store always smelled warm and yeasty, of bread and spices and peace. Sometimes that smell gave her a lump in her throat, and she couldn't say why. It made her think of kitchens where mothers made cookies and put flowers on the table in a pretty jug and braided little girls' hair. Anytime she needed reassurance, or comfort, or a cure for an ailment, or just a loaf of bread, she made a trip to Wing's. And not just for the herbs or the aromas, but for Wing himself, full of advice and wise sayings that she sometimes even understood. Once he'd asked her what the sound of one hand clapping was, and she'd spent days trying to figure that out before she'd finally given up.

"I have a new boarder," she told him.

"Man all in black? Big black horse? Scar?" He handed her a cup of tea.

"That's him. How did you know?"

"Saw him ride in."

"Says he's here on business. You know anything about that?"

He shook his head. "Grubstake suddenly very interesting to strangers."

"So we need to find out what's going on, don't we? How are we going to do that?"

"Usual way. Listen. Observe. Think."

Doesn't snooping have any place in this scheme?
Arley wondered. It was so much easier and faster.

"Snooping is questionable," Wing said.

"Who said anything about snooping?"

"The face is the mirror of the mind," he said, and went back to grinding a knobby brown root with his big marble mortar and pestle.

Arley didn't see how her freckles, straight brows over big brown eyes, and round cheeks could give away anything, but Wing saw things in a way no one else did.

"You ever think of writing down all those things you're always saying?" she asked him. "You could sell them along with your bread and herbs."

"Can hardly *give* advice away. You think people want to pay for it?"

"You'd have to dress it up somehow. Make it more fun. Or pretty." *Or at least understandable,* she thought. "But never mind about that. We have to find out what's going on here."

"It will be revealed."

"Oh, Wing, I wish you'd cut that out. I need some real help."

"You see? No one wants free advice. How to make them pay for it?"

"That's not the advice I want," she said, pouting.

"Then perhaps snooping *will* be necessary." He took a pan of cookies from the oven and slid them onto a plate. "A man's possessions reveal his intentions."

"You think so?" She had in mind Purvis's pile of misspelled mottos, Outdoor John's dead animals, and Prairie Martin's wax gnomes. What in the world did all that say about their intentions?

"If you know how to see," Wing said, handing her a cookie.

"Oh, swell. What if I don't know how?"

"When one is ready to learn, the teacher appears." He went back to work with the mortar and pestle. "You need bread?"

"Two loaves."

She paid for them and went back across the muddy street, concentrating so hard on her snooping assignment she didn't even notice the mules that she absentmindedly shoved aside.

FIVE

MAYBE ARLEY COULD FIND out something about Morgan from Everdene. The miners told Everdene many secrets—right after they fell in love with her, which usually happened within ten minutes of meeting her. Or maybe Bridget knew something. She got information as she waited tables and theoretically cleaned the hotel rooms. "Theoretically" because, until Charles Randall, the hotel hadn't had a guest for over a year—and that guy only stayed because he got off the train to stretch his legs, got to talking to Everdene, and missed the train. It was a whole month before the next train came through, and by then Everdene was so fed up with his lovesick attentions that she marched him to the station at gunpoint to make sure he got on the train and stayed on.

Mid-afternoon was a slow time at the Spittoon. Later in the day miners would come in from their underground toils to spend what little they had managed to prospect or to drown their disappointments, but for now Everdene and Bridget were sitting on stools at the bar drinking sarsaparilla and chatting away like magpies.

Arley couldn't think of two people she'd rather spend time with, which was lucky because they were it when it came to having girlfriends. Gradually every other woman in town, except the Bernaises, had left with their husbands, broke and disgusted or lucky and itchy-footed. The Bernaises stayed, Arley had heard, because Mrs. Bernaise needed the mountain air for her health.

Bridget had arrived as the result of a miner who had hit one big vein, sent for a young Irish mail-order bride as a way of avoiding any goldiggers he might encounter, and then never found another ounce of anything but rocks in his mine. By the time Bridget arrived, her husband-to-be was long gone and there she was, trapped in Grubstake. Only she didn't see it that way. Bridget always said, "This is the easiest job I ever had. And I'm betting it's a lot easier than being married to a miner would be."

Arley was pretty sure Bridget was right. But she still thought that if Bridget's miner had hung around long enough to meet her—eighteen years old, green-eyed, pink-cheeked, and delectably healthy—he would have happily mined nothing but rocks forever.

"Hey, Lemon Drop," Everdene said when she saw Arley. "We've been waiting for you."

Arley bellied up to the bar. Everdene poured a couple of glugs of sarsaparilla into a mostly clean glass.

"Slow day?" Arley asked.

"As usual. But there's going to be a big good-bye party here tonight," Everdene said. "Several guys leaving—Ed Peavy, and Louie, and Sam, and Barney, and Zeb, of course. They all sold their claims."

"But Zeb's already gone. Headed down the mountain this morning on Billy. Took everything. All he left behind were dust bunnies."

"Oh, the others are gone, too. All of them could hardly wait to get out of here. There's going to be a party anyway. Like Prairie Martin said when I saw him this morning on his way to work, now there won't be any need for all those embarrassing farewells and toasts where you're trying to think of something nice to say about a person you don't have anything nice to say about. You should come, Arley. You need a little fun."

"Fun," Arley mused. "I think I've heard that word before. I'm just not sure what it means."

"Well, come tonight and we'll remind you. Grub-stake's finest will be here. Except Lacey, who's made it clear how beneath her the Spittoon is. But you know the doc will show up. He wouldn't want to miss anything free."

"It's free? Are you treating?"

"Not me. Mr. Charles Randall is buying dinner and drinks for everybody. Bridget and I are about to go over to the Eat 'n' Run and help them build up the fire for the barbecue."

"Now, why would he do that?"

"Because he wants to convince everybody else to sell their claims so he can make beautiful downtown Grubstake into a posh resort?" Everdene asked.

Arley turned to Bridget. "Any ideas?"

Bridget shrugged. "Probably for some reason we wouldn't like if we knew what it was. But since we don't, we might as well take the advantage until we do."

"So you think he's up to something, too."

"No question," Bridget said.

"And sooner or later," Everdene added, "we'll know

what it is. We can get mad then. In the meantime, let's eat free barbecue and drink free sarsaparilla."

It made sense. And it meant Arley, for once, wouldn't have to make supper, which was reason enough. "Okay. I'll be here. Oh. I have a new boarder."

"Tall, dark, handsome, and scarred, on a beautiful black horse?" Bridget asked.

"That's him. He says Morgan is the only name he's got. The horse only has one, too—Millicent."

"Better than Zeb in every way I can see," Bridget said.

"You know anything about him?"

"Just that he rode into town, didn't come on the train. Didn't stop at the hotel, but went straight to you."

"He came straight to me? How did he know Zeb had left? How did he know I had a vacancy? And what's with all the strangers?"

"Barbecue first," Everdene reminded her. "Answers second."

But Arley was on a roll. "And what about those crates? Do they belong to Charles Randall? What's in them? Do you know?"

"They do belong to Mr. Randall, and they're dogs," Everdene said.

"Pretty bad-tempered ones, I'd say, from all the

growling," Bridget put in. "And he keeps them in a separate room that I refuse to go in to clean, so he's even going to do that, too."

"What's so special about them?" Arley asked.

"I swear, Lemon Drop, you always did have more questions than I've got answers. Mr. Randall, he's not talking about anything but mines and money, but I'm betting those dogs aren't just precious pets."

"What else could they be?"

"Barbecue first," Everdene said.

—◦◦◉◦·◦◉◦◦—

That night the saloon was full again. Two big events in two nights were a lot for the Grubs, but they were having no trouble getting into the swing. Even Mrs. Bernaise arrived on the doctor's arm, though Lacey had kept her word and stayed away. The Bernaises loitered with great superiority at the back of the room, sipping rotgut as if it were champagne and eating as many of the herb biscuits Wing had brought as they could get hold of.

Already there had been two fights, one cussing match, and a broken nose suffered from falling off a barstool. And that was all before the barbecue was dished up.

"I just hope nobody gets themselves plugged to-night," Everdene said. "Bloodstains are so hard to get out of these plank floors."

"Lemon juice," Bridget said, collecting a tray of mugs. "That does it. Too bad we don't have any lemons." And she whisked off with her burden.

Bridget had been a maid in some fine Irish homes (blood had apparently been spilled in at least one of them) before she'd gotten sick of being ordered around by people too lazy to pick up their own underwear and socks. Then she'd advertised herself as a mail-order bride. At least that way she'd be cleaning up her own house, she figured.

Across the room, leaning smugly against the wall with his hands in his pockets, was Charles Randall, surveying his party. Arley went over to stand next to him. "Nice party," she said.

"My pleasure. You can see how Grubstake could make a fine vacation destination. We'll have to change the name, of course."

"Of course," Arley said, restraining herself from kicking him in the shins. *Grubstake* fit this place perfectly. Taking a deep breath and a flying risk she said, "Pretty amazing what's in those mines, huh?"

Charles Randall came off the wall as though he'd

been pushed from behind. He turned to face Arley with a look that had her backing away from him. "Where did you hear about that?" he growled. "Has Morgan been talking?"

"Morgan?" she squeaked.

"What did he tell you?"

Over Charles Randall's shoulder, Arley could see Morgan coming through the front door of the Spittoon. *Bridget might be wishing she had some lemons pretty soon,* she thought.

Arley pointed. "He...he just came in. Why don't you ask him?" And she whirled away to run up the stairs as soon as Charles Randall turned to look for Morgan. Upstairs she leaned over the banister and watched as the two came together in the midst of the reveling miners, who were paying no attention to anything but refills on beer and barbecue. Charles Randall was speaking so fast he was practically spitting. And Morgan kept shaking his head.

Then the two of them looked around—for her, she was afraid. Arley ducked back from the railing and stood in the dark upstairs hall, her heart pounding so hard she thought she should be able to see the front of her dress move up and down. What the heck had she stumbled onto? What *was* in the mines that Charles

Randall and his boss—whoever that was—were so anxious to have? What was his connection to Morgan? What did Morgan know? And most important, what were they going to do to her now that she'd opened her big mouth?

Well, it's not like *she* could leave town, so she might as well go down and face them in the middle of the party. What could they do to her there? She braced back her shoulders and started down the stairs.

Morgan spotted her first. The men were coming toward her when three miners waylaid Charles Randall to talk about their mines. Morgan kept going. He was on the third step and coming up fast before she knew it.

"So, Miss Arley Pickett," he said in his deadly calm voice. "What have you been saying to Mr. Randall about me?"

When she tried to take a step backward, he grabbed her arm.

"Ow!" she yelped, trying and failing to jerk out of his grasp. "What do you mean? I didn't say anything about you to him."

"And what do you know about the mines?"

"Nothing. They're just mines with not much in them as far as I can tell. At least nobody I know is finding anything. And I know everybody in town."

"You better tell me exactly what you said to him about those mines."

Normally, Arley could lie under pressure, but she didn't think this was the best time for creativity. Well, there was always the truth to fall back on.

"What I said was, 'Pretty amazing what's in those mines.'" She couldn't tell him that she'd said what she'd said just to see how Charles Randall would react. "All I meant was that it's amazing he's paying all that money for mines that are so worthless. There's nothing in them. That's the amazing part." Was he buying this? And if he was, could she sell it to Charles Randall, too? She opened her eyes a little wider, wishing she'd paid more attention to how Lacey did that, even though, really, it was enough to make you gag.

"Why are you making that face?" Morgan asked.

"What face?" She blinked her eyes which, unfortunately, wasn't the same as batting them.

"Do you have something in your eye?"

"No," she said grumpily, giving up on the eye maneuvers. "I didn't mean anything, I swear. I was just making conversation."

With the arm that wasn't holding Arley, Morgan beckoned to Charles Randall. He came steaming across the room through the oblivious miners, who considered a party too important an event to be interrupted by somebody who appeared to be in a plain old bad mood. Now, if he was looking for a fight, that was different. That would be part of the entertainment.

Arley had to steel herself not to cringe in the face of Charles Randall's approach. Cringing was a bad way to begin any conversation. Besides, she was getting mad now herself. What *was* in those mines that was causing these strangers to get themselves in such an uproar? What were they trying to put over on the Grubs anyway?

"So, young lady," Charles Randall began.

"So yourself," she retaliated. She was much better at righteous indignation, even fake righteous indignation (though she was getting into it enough now that it didn't feel fake anymore), than she was at the eyelash stuff. "What's the big idea getting after me like that when all I was doing was making pleasant chit-chat? I was just saying it was amazing that those worthless mines could get sold."

He stopped, frowning. "That's not what you said." But he didn't sound so sure. "You said it was amazing what was *in* the mines."

"There's *nothing* in those mines," she scoffed. "Everybody knows that. Why else did you think all those guys were so ready to sell out?"

"I know you said something about what's *in* the mines."

"There's *nothing* in the mines." She sounded entirely exasperated. She *was* exasperated.

"And you said Morgan told you something."

Arley drew herself up to another six degrees of indignation even though it was hard with Morgan still holding her arm. "I *never* said that. You're the one who mentioned Morgan. I didn't even know you *knew* Morgan." Though by now she was *sure* Charles Randall was the reason Morgan hadn't wanted to stay at the hotel.

"Well, we...ah...we've met." Suddenly Charles Randall sounded disconcerted. "Perhaps this has all been a terrible misunderstanding."

"I should say so," Arley said, shaking her arm again, and this time Morgan let her go. "And I must say, I don't appreciate being unjustly accused, especially of something I didn't do. Oh—I guess that's the unjust part. Anyway, that, and also being yelled at and insulted *and* manhandled." Actually the manhandling hadn't been so bad now that it was over. Even if Morgan *was* in cahoots with Charles Randall—and it sure looked like he was—how often did she have a handsome though menacing young man putting his hands on her? She could have been in a scene right out of *Pamela's Predicament.* "I think you owe me an apology." She straightened her sleeve. "Both of you."

Morgan and Charles Randall looked at each other, then at Arley.

"Oh, all *right,*" Charles Randall finally said. "I'm... I'm...what happened shouldn't have happened. I suppose."

She wanted to say, "You call that an apology?" but thought maybe she should quit while she was ahead, especially since he was still regarding her in a suspicious way. She turned her scowling face to Morgan, waiting.

"I hope I didn't hurt you," he said.

His scowl matched her own but he did sound sorry. Maybe he was as good at faking emotion as she was. She also recognized that wasn't an apology either, not really, but somehow it affected her in a way Charles Randall's nonapology hadn't. At the least, it seemed more personal.

"Well. Not too much. But I'll probably be bruised. A little." She trailed off. "I need a drink." She elbowed her way past them and through the miners, barely making it to the bar where she had something to hang on to. For some reason her knees felt watery.

"Hey, Arley," Everdene said. She was so busy behind the bar she looked like she had five arms. "Want a drink?"

"Give me two."

"Two sarsaparillas?"

"Two anythings."

"I think the way you look, it better be sarsaparilla. Does wanting two of them have anything to do with what was going on between you and Morgan and Charles Randall? I was about to come over there and knock some heads together, but you seemed to be handling it."

"I can't explain it right now. I'll have to tell you tomorrow." She drank down the first sarsaparilla and then the second one, wiped her mouth on her sleeve, and burped loud enough to cause several partyers to turn around and look.

She heaped a plate with barbecue and carried it out through the chilly mountain night to home. On the doorstep she stopped and looked up through breaking clouds at a dazzling sprinkle of stars against the black sky. Did stars look like that in London and New York and Rome and San Francisco? Or just here in funny old Grubstake?

When she opened the door, the dogs, banned from the party for good reason, flung themselves joyously on her, as if she had been gone for weeks. She went down in a furry heap as they licked her, nuzzled her, and stepped on her—and then discovered the barbecue, which they demolished at record speed. Full, and once again used to her, they wandered off to flop down in front of the warm stove to digest.

Arley got to her feet, brushed off the dog hair, and went upstairs to bed.

Six

SOMEHOW ARLEY SLEPT, even knowing that Morgan—mysterious, frightening Morgan—was in a room down the hall, perhaps contemplating murdering her in her bed. Maybe she was calmed by knowing that she'd pushed her bureau up against her door. Which made a problem the next morning when she tried to move it. The bureau was heavier when she wasn't all pumped up with anxiety and sarsaparilla, and she was late getting down to breakfast.

"Where's our new fella?" Outdoor John asked.

"I have no idea," Arley snapped. "If he's not here at breakfast time, he doesn't get breakfast. That's the rule."

"We know, we know," Outdoor John said, not wanting to jeopardize his own breakfast.

Arley's mood caused them to leave for their mines earlier than they normally did. No lingering over coffee and tall tales this morning. Though for once she wouldn't have minded. She didn't relish being alone when Morgan appeared. She tried to keep the dogs in with her, but they threw themselves against the kitchen door in their eagerness to begin their own activities, until finally she had to let them out.

Just as she shut the door after them she heard boots on the stairs.

"Morgan," she muttered. "He better not be thinking about breakfast."

"Good morning," he said, coming into the room all shaved and washed, smelling good (a novelty all by itself) and looking sinister. "I see I've missed breakfast."

"There's coffee on the stove," she said. And then, to her dismay, she heard herself say, "The griddle's still hot. I can make you some flapjacks." A hot pan could make a good weapon, she reasoned, but why was she cooking for him at all? Why wasn't she sending him off to the Eat 'n' Run where he could get indigestion, like everybody else who ate there? Even fear was no excuse for acting like such a pinhead.

"Thank you." He sat and silently watched her cook.

While he ate, Arley washed the dishes in water she'd heated on the stove. When he finished his flapjacks, he brought her his plate and picked up a towel to dry what she'd already washed. Having him stand so close to her made her stomach feel all fluttery.

"You don't need to do that."

"I was taught I should be grateful enough for my meal that I was willing to help clean up after it."

How could somebody with such a sensible upbringing turn out rotten enough to be in cahoots with Charles Randall?

"Well. Okay." But accepting his offer made her feel so panicky, she ended up juggling a soapy teacup so expertly that she could have qualified for the circus. After they'd finished the washing-up in silence, he said, "I'll see you at supper time," and left.

Arley was about to sink down with a cup of tea and *Pamela's Predicament* when she changed her mind and charged out the door on her way to the Spittoon. She had her own predicament to worry about. Once again she forgot her bonnet and this time she also forgot to take off her apron.

Naturally she ran into Lacey as soon as she stepped from the muddy street to the wooden sidewalk in front of the general store.

"Well, good morning, Arley," Lacey said, as fresh and fluffy as a valentine. "Don't you look...well..." and she cocked her head and smiled. "It's a beautiful morning, isn't it?"

"I guess so," Arley said, glumly eyeing the gray drizzly sky.

"I'm buying sugar. Mama and I are baking today. Little cakes. We're having a tea party this afternoon."

A tea party. While Arley would be chopping up fatback for the beans. "That's nice."

"Duncan's coming. He loves Mama's cakes." She fussed with the bow on her bonnet. "Duncan's very sweet, don't you think?"

"I suppose." What a twit. Duncan was more than sweet. He was a *crusader.* What did she think being a newspaperman was all about—reporting on the activities of a couple of dogs? The newspaper was a forum, a place where an important voice could be heard. It wasn't his fault nothing big ever happened in Grubstake. If it did, Duncan would be ready, Arley just knew it, no matter what his father had thought. What she couldn't figure out was why Duncan had the slightest interest in Lacey. Whatever brains she might have underneath all those blond curls seemed devoted to apparel, games of piquet, and fussing over Fifi. She certainly wouldn't know what an escutcheon was. Could it be that Duncan found her company restful after all his hard mental work?

"He's quite eligible, too," Lacey said.

"Eligible for what?"

"Well, for marriage, of course." Lacey fiddled with her gloves.

"Marriage? You want to marry Duncan?"

Lacey did that thing with her eyelashes. "Well. A lady would never say that."

Who makes up these rules? Arley wondered. *Why couldn't people just say what they thought?* It would make things so much simpler, and eliminate all the guessing you had to do, like now, when you weren't sure what was going on. "If you weren't such a *lady,* what would you say?"

"It's been nice talking to you, Arley," Lacey said with a little sniff and swept off into the store.

Could Duncan be interested enough in Lacey to actually marry her? Was there a way Arley could tell him what a train wreck that would be? *Probably not something a lady would do,* she snorted, and went on down the sidewalk to the Spittoon.

Bridget was on her hands and knees scrubbing the floor.

"I hope that's not lemon juice," Arley said.

Bridget looked up and smiled. "Just soap and water. No blood got spilled, though plenty of barbecue sauce and beer did."

Arley looked around. Tables were pushed out of the way, chairs were on their sides, the bar was littered with dirty mugs, and there was somebody lying motionless on the floor at the foot of the stairs.

Arley asked, pointing, "Is that Mickey? Is he okay?"

Bridget looked over her shoulder at the livery operator. "Oh. Yes. We didn't want to disturb him, him being so sound asleep and all. So we just left the mess and went off to bed last night. The thing about messes, you know, is they don't clean themselves up. They wait for you."

"That's what I want to talk to you and Everdene about."

"Messes?"

"The one with Charles Randall and Morgan in it. Whatever's going on here, they're in it together."

Everdene had come up behind Arley.

"I agree, Lemon Drop. I saw the two of them with you last night, and I watched them after you left, too. They're definitely not strangers. But I don't think they like each other."

"Me, neither," Arley said.

"So how are we going to find out what's going on?"

Bridget sat back on her heels, the scrub brush in her hand. "There's only two ways. We follow and eavesdrop and pick up little clues and take forever piecing things painstakingly together, or we snoop in their rooms."

Arley was so grateful that Bridget had learned plenty of useful tricks from working for all those rich families.

"Mr. Randall is still upstairs, snoozing I presume," Everdene said, "so there's no possibility of following him and no chance to snoop on him. We'll have to concentrate on Morgan. You know where he is?"

"He left after breakfast." Arley would remove her own eyeball with a rusty spoon before she'd admit she'd made him special late-breakfast flapjacks. "I don't know where he went."

"I saw him go by on that big horse of his," Bridget said. "Headed toward the mines."

Arley swallowed hard. She was all for following him, no question about that, but only as long as he didn't actually go inside a mine. Ever since her father had dynamited himself out of his own mine in that impressive (though, unfortunately, fatal) loop-the-loop, she had been terrified of being inside a mine. She knew it had probably been his own carelessness that had caused the explosion, but it didn't have to be. Maybe the Indian spirits who lived in the mountains thought her father's heart wasn't pure enough for him to be messing with their natural resources. Arley hadn't had her own heart assayed lately, but her inclination toward fibbing and snooping probably wasn't a good sign. She wasn't interested in taking a chance on meeting a peeved spirit underground. Besides, there were flammable gasses in mines, and cave-ins and bats and ... well, it was dark, too.

She was willing to butcher her own meat, cut down her own trees, even sew her own clothes, but she wasn't willing to go in after her own gold. Not that in her lifetime there'd been much gold from the Never Mine to get excited about. All the good stuff, which had allowed her father to build the house that now supported her (thank goodness), had been found before she was born.

"So who wants to go look?" Everdene asked.

"Where?" Arley asked. "There's mines all over the place up there. How can we know which one he's in? Or even if he's in one at all. And won't it seem suspicious if somebody sees one of us peeking into mines?"

"Then how are we supposed to figure out what he's doing?" Everdene asked.

Arley scratched her head. And her conscience.

Which ignored her. "Well, I could do some casual snooping. He's gone, we know that, so his room is empty for a while. I could go in there to dust."

"You could even dust the insides of his drawers, couldn't you?" Bridget asked.

"Why, Bridget," Arley said. "Did you do that in the houses where you worked?"

She shrugged. "The insides of drawers need dusting from time to time. Everybody knows that. People with things to hide shouldn't keep them in their drawers."

"That makes perfect sense to me," Arley said. "And you know what? The insides of those drawers haven't been dusted in a long, long time. I'd better get moving."

"You've already got your apron on, so you're ready."

Arley looked down at herself. "Oh, rats. I forgot. And I stood out there talking to Lacey Bernaise looking like this! I swear she makes me feel like . . . well, like Mickey over there." She gestured to where Mickey still lay, one boot off (and a hole in the toe of his exposed sock), his shirttail out, his hair standing up (though he wasn't) in cowlicks. "She's wanting to marry Duncan, did you know that?" Arley swallowed. "What do you think her chances are?"

Everdene spoke up. "I think it would be a catastrophe. For both of them."

"But you think that about everybody's romantic possibilities," Arley said. "They're all catastrophes-in-waiting."

"True. One thing I've learned for sure is you can't tell a person in love anything. Not a single thing. Their brains don't work at all."

"So, you think they're..."—she could hardly force out the words—"in love?"

"Sounds like Lacey is. Or at least in love with matrimony. As for Duncan, I have no idea. He seems to spend a fair amount of time over there, but maybe he just needs a decent meal. Dolly Bernaise is a good cook, and poor old Duncan must get tired of fixing for himself since his father disappeared. That was hard on Duncan. Oh, I know they had their problems, but Sebastian really did have faith that Duncan would someday come into his own, even if he never told Duncan that. But that Lacey's a determined girl when she sets her mind on something. Remember when she wanted that palomino pony her daddy said was too expensive? He's living in their barn right this minute, and I don't mean her daddy."

"So you think Duncan's," Arley swallowed hard, "done for?"

Everdene laughed. "Your view of matrimony seems

to be about the same as mine. Well, no, I don't think he's done for. Yet. He's a fellow with some gumption, and he may be able to avoid her. If he wants to."

"You think she wants you to tell Duncan what she said?" Bridget asked. "Kind of prepare the way? Are you going to?"

"Are you kidding?" Arley said. "I don't want those words in my mouth one more time."

Everdene laughed and said, "Arley, you better get going instead of hanging around here jawing about Miss Lacey. You've got some dusting to do."

"You're right. But... what if he comes back while I'm in there? And—oh—I forgot—he's locked the door."

"No problem," Bridget said, taking a hairpin from her ginger-colored topknot. "I'll show you how to fix that. Follow me."

She led Arley up the stairs, past Charles Randall's room and the room next door from which growling could be heard, to the vacant room at the end of the hall. She removed a key from her pocket and locked the door. "Test the door. It's locked, right?"

Arley tried the very locked door. "Yep."

"Now watch." Bridget inserted her hairpin into the lock, wiggled it around until a tiny click sounded, turned the knob, and the door opened.

"Why, that's wonderful!" Arley exclaimed. "Teach me."

Just as Arley was springing the lock for the fourth time to make sure she really knew how, Charles Randall's door opened and he stood there, resplendent in a green linen suit, watching them. "What are you doing?" he asked.

"Well, we're...we're checking on the hardware. Seeing what needs polishing or replacing or whatnot," Bridget lied smoothly. Arley could only look on with admiration.

"Looked to me like you were picking that lock."

"Why, sir," Bridget said, drawing herself up in outrage. "How can you suggest such a thing? We work hard to keep our reputations spotless—a difficult job, as you might imagine, in this place."

"Hmmm, yes," he said, and started downstairs.

Bridget and Arley crouched in the dark upstairs hall, their hands over their mouths to keep from giggling. Bridget peeked through the hall railings to make sure Charles Randall had left the hotel before handing Arley an extra hairpin and saying, "Good luck."

As Arley ran down the stairs, she called back, "I'm glad you're using your powers for good!"

SEVEN

ARLEY CARRIED HER DUST CLOTH, pail, broom, and scrub brush upstairs with her so she'd look as if she actually were cleaning if Morgan came home early. She stood outside his room waiting to see if her heartbeat would quit galloping. You only locked your door if you had a secret, right? She took some deep breaths, decided her heart wasn't going to cooperate, and stuck the hairpin into the keyhole. A few wiggles and the door was unlocked. She stood in the hall for a long, long moment, admiring her new accomplishment, before she summoned up the pluck to actually open the door.

True, he'd only been in the room for a day, but it looked as if it were still vacant. The bed was tautly made. There was nothing new except for the saddle-bags on the floor by the window, and the shaving brush, strop, and razor on the washstand. Not that she'd expected him to add embroidered pillows and family portraits, but shouldn't there be *something*? Dirty socks on the floor, a book, a personal item? It seemed that he was hiding even himself.

Arley opened the top drawer of the bureau. Shirts and underwear. Normal male possessions, except maybe for the underwear, which some of her boarders had had to be convinced was a necessity in her house if they were going to sit on her chairs. And all the clothes were black. What was that about? Was he in mourning? A mortician? Someone with no imagination?

The second drawer seemed to be stuck. She wrestled with it for a minute before it finally pulled open to reveal many books. Many very heavy books. No wonder it had hurt to kick that saddlebag. She began lifting them out. *Geology of the Mountain West, Schists and Basalts, Geoclines, Sedimentary Secrets. Ah,* she thought. A title worthy of a Penny Dreadful. That last author had some idea of how to attract a reader.

Okay, so maybe Morgan was a person who studied rocks. Which is what mines were full of. So there had to be something important in those rocks, or what was he doing here, with all those books? And it probably wasn't gold or silver or lead because the miners of Grubstake would have found any of those after all these years of trying. What else could it be? No one had ever found any traces of copper or tin or even salt in this area. Could it be diamonds? Oooh, that would be nice. But wouldn't somebody have noticed that? Didn't they sparkle, even in the dark?

Arley replaced the books exactly as she'd found them—she hoped—and shoved the drawer shut. The bottom drawer was full of papers—drawings of what looked like cross-sections of mountains with notations in small, elegant handwriting—"strong possibility" and "negligible amounts likely"; lists of latitude and longitude locations; and letters on Lockwood Ltd. letterhead.

The first letter had to do with travel directions for getting to Grubstake. It included letters of credit and was signed by A. Jackson, Comptroller. The second letter was signed by Charles Randall and was about the resort that they were going to make out of Grubstake. Except that the word resort was always in quotation marks. The last two lines of the letter said, "Your reputation for utmost discretion may be tested. Do not fail the test."

There was one more letter, signed by Mr. Sidney Lockwood himself, expressing confidence in Morgan—

just Morgan, no last name, exactly as he'd said—and his ability to make sure that what they suspected was actually a fact and telling him that his rewards could be great if everything Lockwood Ltd. hoped to accomplish could, in fact, be accomplished. The letter went on to say that the punishment for failure would be great, especially if it made Mr. Lockwood look bad, which was the worst crime an employee—or anybody else—could commit.

Mr. Lockwood sounded like an egotistical blockhead. A *dangerous* egotistical blockhead. Why would anybody want to work for somebody like that? Unless Morgan was another dangerous... well, maybe she shouldn't think about that right now.

A sudden sound made her straighten up, alert. Was Morgan returning early? She cast a frantic glance at the window, a possible escape route except that it was twenty-five feet off the ground.

The sound came again. And again, as Arley's heartbeat accelerated. Then the sound was followed by a howl and she knew what it was: the dogs throwing themselves against the door, wanting to be let in.

She leaned against the wall in relief. They could just wait a few minutes, the impatient mutts!

She scrabbled around in the drawer, hoping she was leaving no indication of scrabbling. There had to be *something* that wasn't so darn *oblique* that would clarify what Morgan was up to. But there was nothing else except a box of dog biscuits. He ate dog biscuits? She shrugged. Maybe they were good. Orville and Wilbur had never had such a luxury, so how would she know? Arley took one from the box and sniffed it. It smelled like...like dirt. She could see how that would be appealing to a dog. She tried to break off a small piece to sample, but the thing was hard as stone. So she licked it, just to see how it tasted. Yuck! It just confirmed her belief that dogs will eat anything. She pocketed a couple of biscuits for Wilbur and Orville, as compensation for being kept waiting, replaced the box, patted the papers back into place, and smacked shut the drawer in frustration.

There was nothing under the bed, or under the pillows, and nothing in the saddlebags except a poncho and a block of chewing tobacco. Ugh. She hated chewing tobacco. Her boarders were forbidden to use it, not in the house, not anywhere. All that drooling, and brown juice, and spitting. Ugh! Morgan seemed too clean to use the stuff, but maybe it was a requirement for bad guys, along with all their other bad habits.

Arley relocked the door and lugged her cleaning equipment downstairs, relieved to get out of there without getting caught. She'd learned nothing except that Lockwood Ltd.—whatever that was—was some-how involved. She still didn't know what was in the mines, or why it was important, or just how worried all the Grubs should be. If ever she'd needed a dose of *Pamela's Predicament,* it was now. But somehow Pamela's predicament was looking pretty tame compared to her own.

Maybe Wing could shed some of his murky light on the situation. This time she remembered to put on her bonnet and take off her apron before she let the dogs in and left the house.

—◦◦◎◦◦—

"Hi, Wing. What's cooking?"

"Donuts. You want one?"

"Sure." It was light and fluffy and fresh—everything Arley wasn't. "Last night at the farewell party I found out that Charles Randall and that new guy with the scar and the great horse, Morgan, know each other. They both work for a company called Lockwood Ltd., and they're after something in the mines that we don't know anything about. What do you know about geology?"

"Not much."

"Got any guesses about what might be in our mines?"

Wing shrugged. "Diamonds? Rubies? Emeralds?"

"But don't they sparkle? Wouldn't somebody have noticed?"

He lifted one shoulder inscrutably. "In China, most precious thing to find in a mine is blue jade. Long time ago, used to make burial suits out of squares of blue jade tied together with gold or silver wire. Supposed to keep body from decaying. Chinese saying goes, 'There is a price for gold, but there is no price for jade.'"

"I never heard of blue jade. Do you think we have some here?"

"Doubt it. Blue jade too rare to be commercial. But interesting. These guys, they want something big. Something commercial."

"Maybe it's some special ore, something with a particular use that we don't know anything about. Something like stibnite or cassiterite."

"Never heard of those."

"Duncan wrote an article for the paper once about ores. I remember them."

"You remember? Words like that?"

Arley flushed. "Well, yeah. He's an excellent writer. Memorable. Very—". and then she stopped herself, self-consciously aware of the way Wing was looking at her with his bright inquisitive eyes. "Well," she said primly, folding her hands on the counter in front of her. "Maybe it's something like that."

"Snooping no help then?" he asked, dropping more dough into the hot fat.

"How did you know I'd—" She stopped and took a deep breath. "My sources are confidential but so far they've not revealed this critical piece of information. Ever heard of Lockwood Ltd.?"

"Helped build our railroad. Big company, lots of parts. Railroads, land, mining, forestry, things tycoons interested in. Sidney Lockwood the big boss. What he most interested in is making money. He always looking for new ways. He have all sorts of experts working for him, looking for those ways."

He fished out the donuts and put them to drain on the most recent copy of the *Expositor*. "He have reputation for ruthlessness. Well deserved. Good man to stay away from."

"Great," Arley said, helping herself to another donut. "Yet another terrible person is involved with whatever's going on here." With her mouth full, she said, "How are we supposed to figure this out? We're just us."

"Many heads can make one thought."

"I think we need a few more heads, then, because the ones we've got working on this aren't getting anywhere."

"Don't need more heads. Need more information."

"We've got a shortage of that, too."

"Take some donuts home. Maybe Mr. Morgan like to have one with cup of coffee and chat with you."

"You want me to pump him for information face to face over donuts? The guy with the scar and the black wardrobe and the one name? Are you nuts?"

"When devious means fail, try straightforward ones."

"Oh, sure. Easy for you to say."

"Not so easy. 'Straightforward' is very hard word in English."

—◦—◦⊛◦⊛◦—◦—

Arley went home with a dozen donuts wrapped in a copy of the *Expositor* and a gallon of anxiety in her heart, dreading the return of her newest boarder.

It happened sooner than she was prepared for. She'd just washed up her lunch dishes when she heard the front door open. She came out into the hall drying her hands on her apron.

"Oh, it's you," she said, trying to sound casual when she saw Morgan.

"Yes," he said, starting up the stairs.

"There's coffee on the stove if you want some." She added, "It's fresh." Then she turned and headed back to the kitchen, half-hoping he wouldn't follow her.

Behind her she heard his footsteps but didn't look at him until she was right next to the stove.

"It smells good," he said, rubbing his hands together to warm them.

Arley snatched the coffeepot off the stovetop and poured two cups.

"You're joining me?" he asked.

"Sure. I've been out, too, and it's still cold, even though it's supposed to be spring. Funny how the weather is up here." She rattled on about Grubstake's lousy weather as she set out sugar and cream and the plate of donuts, sounding even to herself like a perfect nincompoop. "I guess this'll have to be a resort for people who like to be cold and wet. Have a seat," she said.

He sat and took the hot cup between his hands, causing her to notice how strong they looked, capable of snapping a neck in an instant. She gulped, and poured sugar and cream into her coffee. Naturally he took his black and bitter, probably like his soul.

"So. How...how was your day?" she asked.

"All right. Yours?"

"All right. I—" She couldn't tell him she'd been rummaging through his things and then had gone to see Wing, so she blundered ahead with "—went to the Spittoon to help clean up. That was quite a messy party last night."

"I've seen messier."

She envisioned ones involving plenty of spilled body fluids, and took a quick swallow of too-hot coffee. "Ow, ow, ow!" She gulped, jumping up to pour a glass of water from the pitcher on the work table. She stood, guzzling it, hoping she'd still be able to produce speech once the fire went out.

"You all right?" he asked. Maybe it was her imagination, but he seemed to be trying not to laugh.

Her tongue felt thick and inflexible, and it hurt, but she nodded. "Fine. Fine. Have a donut."

Morgan looked at the plate for a long time before he selected one.

"Did you make these?" he asked. Studying him as he studied the donuts, with his face relaxed, she was able to see that he was younger than she'd first thought. Probably around Duncan's age.

Oh, what the heck, she thought. "Yes. Do you like donuts?"

He looked hard at the one in his hand before taking a small bite. He chewed, swallowed, and said, "That's the best donut I ever tasted. When I was a kid, getting a donut was as rare as striking gold, and just as glorious."

Donuts were as good as gold? Well, he *was* interested in geology, but that comparison seemed kind of extreme. "Well, we got plenty of them around here. Have another one. How's your business coming along?"

He ate the second donut and drank some coffee. "My business would be *my* business, now, wouldn't it?"

Arley's tongue already felt as strange as if it belonged to somebody else, so she plunged ahead. "It's got to have something to do with the mines, that's obvious. We're not stupid, you know. Well, some of us are, I guess. Most of us, maybe. At least some of the time—oh, never mind that. It's just that that's all Charles Randall's interested in buying. We don't *have* to be geniuses to figure out the mines are important."

Dang. She was doing all the talking, telling him more than he was telling her. Maybe she *was* one of the stupid ones.

Under his breath she heard him mutter, "I told him this was a mistake." At least that's what she thought she heard.

Morgan stood up. "Thanks for the coffee."

As he started out of the kitchen, she said, "Would you like another donut?"

He stopped, but didn't turn around. After a long pause, she watched him set his shoulders. "No, thank you," he said, and continued on out and then up the stairs.

Arley sank her chin into her hand and drank some more water to cool her tongue. Phooey. All she knew was that he loved donuts. And that he was disciplined enough to turn them down when he needed to. Guess he'd shown her who was in charge around here.

While she sat there she heard his boots on the stairs. Was he going out *again*? Was it because of something she'd said? She stood. Maybe there was more than one way to get some facts about him.

As soon as Arley heard the front door close, she grabbed her shawl and watched out the front window until she saw him go into the Spittoon. Then she dashed out the door and down the front steps.

The dogs, who had been lounging on the porch, jumped up and trotted after her. They'd scarfed down the dog biscuits in an instant, proving once again that dogs really will eat anything, and were hoping she had more for them.

"Go home!" she said, pointing back at the porch. "Now! Go!"

But they just milled around her, looking up at her with their tongues lolling out, grinning.

"Oh, holy buckets. I've got to go." And she hurried

on to the hotel with the dogs jogging along with her. All three of them came through the doors of the Spittoon, surprising Bridget and Everdene, who sat at a table in the empty room playing Old Maid.

In a whisper, Arley asked, "Did Morgan just come in here?"

"What?" Everdene asked.

Arley whispered louder, pointing up the stairs. "Is Morgan up there?"

"Oh. Yeah. Why are you whispering?"

"I don't want him to know I'm here," she whispered. "I'm following him." She grabbed the dogs by the scruffs of their necks, dragging them to the table. "Can you hang on to them? I've got some eavesdropping to do, and they'd botch it up."

Everdene grabbed Orville's neck, and Bridget took Wilbur's while Arley tiptoed quickly up the stairs, tripping only once on her skirt. From the hall she could hear a rumble of voices coming from Mr. Randall's room. She slipped into the room next to Mr. Randall's—on the other side from the room with the growly dogs. Softly, she closed the door, picked up the water glass from the washstand, and put the open end against the wall. With her ear pressed against the other end, she could hear every word Morgan and

Charles Randall were saying. She felt like cheering. The trick Clarissa used to eavesdrop on her cowboy actually worked in real life.

"I told you these people aren't the bumpkins you think they are," she heard Morgan saying. "They know something's up with those mines."

"Even if they do," Charles Randall said, "they're still willing to sell, so what difference does it make?"

"So far, the ones you've bought are the wrong ones. You've got to buy more. And that's going to be harder now that they're suspicious. Don't you get that?"

Arley was liking how annoyed Morgan sounded with his partner in crime. Friction between thieves was always an interesting development in Penny Dreadfuls.

"My dear Morgan. Are you underestimating my persuasive abilities? You do your part and I'll do mine, which is so much more important than yours. You wouldn't want me telling Mr. Lockwood about your doubts, now, would you? I know how much you need to keep this job, not having any family to fall back on, and all those dependents to support."

"How do you know—?"

"I know everything about you." Charles Randall cut him off. "Mr. Lockwood likes to have some dirt on all his employees. It makes them so much easier to manipulate."

"That means he's got some on you, too."

There was a pause while Charles Randall digested that. "He would if there was any to get. Which there isn't. So I'm not worried," he said, sounding worried.

"Great. You're not worried. I'm happy for you. Just get me some more mines. I'm convinced it's there—all the evidence points to that—but if it's not, we'll have to be moving on. And it would be nice to do it under our own steam and not by being run out of town on a rail."

Suddenly there was a great commotion out in the hall. Barking and howling, growling and scratching.

Oh, no, Arley thought, dropping the glass. It didn't break, so she kicked it under the bed and rushed to the door. She'd recognized some of that racket as Orville and Wilbur.

She got into the hall seconds before Charles Randall and Morgan came busting out of their room. They stared at her for a moment before turning to where Orville and Wilbur stood snarling at a closed door, their hackles so raised they looked twice as fuzzy as normal. Bridget and Everdene had rushed up the stairs, but stood helplessly aside.

"Sorry, Arley," Everdene said. "They made a break for it."

From behind the door came snarls and growls, plus

the sound of claws tearing against wood. Arley had never seen her dogs foaming at the mouth the way they were, or throwing themselves so hard against a door. She'd never been afraid of them before.

"Miss Pickett," Charles Randall said, grabbing her arm. "Control your animals."

She yanked her arm away. "Why don't you control yours? They must have started it."

Just then the door burst open and two little wiener-shaped dogs came tearing out, fangs bared, barking their heads off.

"Brute!" Charles Randall hollered. "Muggs! Stop that! Or else!"

Instantly, the dogs shut up and cowered together, shivering. Even Orville and Wilbur were startled into shutting up, though cowering was definitely not their style. They cocked their heads, jowls still dripping, and stared at Brute and Muggs. Arley felt like cocking her own head and staring, too. But without the drooling. What kind of power did this guy have over those two little dogs? And why were they even here?

"You brought your dogs with you?" she asked. "Why?"

"Not that it's any of your business," Charles Randall said, "but I'm very fond of them. I like to have them with me."

"But they're not with you. They're locked up next door." By now she'd grabbed hold of Orville, and Bridget had dragged Wilbur away from Muggs and Brute.

"So apparently I have better command of my animals than you do of yours. Wouldn't you agree?"

To Arley, Wilbur and Orville were more like relatives than possessions. Dominating them wasn't why she wanted them around.

It was clear she wasn't going to get anything out of Charles Randall, so she said, "I think we'll be going now." She dragged Orville toward the stairs, but Wilbur was resisting Bridget's efforts to do the same with him.

"I can help," Morgan said, taking a handful of Wilbur's fur and pulling him away from Bridget and toward the stairs. Wilbur looked surprised, and then came along cooperatively.

How did Morgan do that? Arley wondered. Maybe he smelled like dog biscuits.

Once they were out on the sidewalk, both dogs trotted companionably along with Morgan, as if they were old friends. Arley had to wonder where dogs had gotten the reputation of being good judges of character.

"What are you, some kind of dog magician?" Arley asked Morgan peevishly. She was too cross to be apprehensive. "They never behave like that for me. How many dogs have you had?"

"None. I move around too much to have one. And I never had one growing up. We couldn't keep pets in the orphanage."

"You grew up in an orphanage?" She remembered he'd said he never knew his parents, but it was hard for her to think of him as an abandoned child. Or as a child at all, really.

"Yes."

"I think that's mean, not to let you have a pet," she told him. "If anybody needs a furry friend, it's an orphan. Orville and Wilbur were a big—well, *help* is too strong a word since they're never really any help—but they were good company when *I* was orphaned. They slept with me every night when I was so lonely and scared."

Morgan gave her a long level look that made her heart stutter in alarm. She didn't think she'd ever seen such thick eyelashes on a man. They made his eyes seem even darker and more fearsome. "Prohibiting pets was hardly the meanest thing that happened there," he said.

"Is that where you—" She pointed to his cheek. Hey. If you wanted to know something, it didn't hurt to ask. Sometimes you got an answer.

"Probably," he said. "I've had it as long as I can remember."

Arley still had trouble thinking of Morgan as a helpless child who could be so terribly abused. But she was at least relieved to know that he hadn't gotten the scar from some regular, sportive violence.

"I'm sorry," she said. "That's awful."

"Yes," he said. "Thank you."

They'd arrived at her house by then, but as Arley opened the front door, allowing the dogs to tear through the parlor with their muddy paws, he put his hand on her arm, causing her to jump a little.

"I won't be with you for supper tonight." Then, after a long pause during which he kept his hand on her arm, and she struggled not to shiver from it, he said, "Are Purvis and Prairie Martin and Outdoor John going to sell their mines?"

"Not if I can help it."

"Good." He let go of her, turned and walked back up the street, a dark figure in the waning mountain light.

Good? she thought, watching him walk away. Wasn't he supposed to *want* the mines, the way Charles Randall did? Oh, this was way more complicated than any Penny Dreadful she'd ever read, where there was always a plot that made sense. She was starting to wonder why she'd ever thought it would be fun if real life was more like a Penny Dreadful.

⟶◦⟨◦⟩·⟨◦⟩◦⟵

Over supper that night, thrown together in a big hurry since she'd spent the day on investigations, Arley exhorted her boarders not to sell their mines.

"That Charles Randall and Morgan, they're in cahoots. They know there might be something valuable in your mines. That's why they want them."

"That's why *we* wanted them, too," Prairie Martin said. "That's the whole idea about mining. And if you can't find what you're looking for, what's the use of hanging on if somebody's willing to offer you good money for the worthless thing? Isn't that what capitalism's all about? Or free enterprise or something like that? Isn't that okay?"

"But what if somebody else found something very valuable in your mine after you sold it? Wouldn't you feel bad?"

"I don't know. I guess so. But what if the money from the sale let me go do something else I'd like better?"

"And what would that be?" Oh, it wasn't nice to ask that question of somebody who had such a hard time making up his mind, but she was tired of this conversation. She'd managed to hardly think about mines for the last couple of years, even though she owned one, and now that's almost all she *did* think about.

"If we sold out, would we have to leave Grubstake?" Outdoor John wrinkled his brow.

"I suppose not." It suddenly occurred to her that without boarders she'd have no income—never mind that her current income was mostly theoretical. Holy catfish, why hadn't she thought about that before? She had more than curiosity motivating her now to prevent the mine sales.

"Arley," Purvis asked. "You sure you ain't been reading too many of those books you get from the train? Seems like maybe you're imagining some things that ain't doing nothing but worrying us all. Too much reading can be bad for your mind. You do know that, right?"

"This has nothing to do with my Penny Dreadfuls—and my mind is just fine, thank you. Just hang on a little while longer. Please. It's important. And remember who does the laundry and the cooking and the sewing on of buttons around here." She gave each of them one of her hardest stares.

EIGHT

THE NEXT MORNING, as soon as the breakfast dishes
were done, Arley yanked off her apron, rushed out
the kitchen door, then rushed back in to stand before
the little mirror by the coat tree in the hall. "Oh!" she
exclaimed. "I look like I haven't combed my hair for
months! I look like I've been pulled through a hedge
backwards! What happens to my head when all I do
with it is practically nothing?" She pushed and pulled
at her curls for a minute, but they resisted any kind
of organization. "Oh, well, that'll have to be good
enough," she said, giving her unruly mop a final pat
and setting off again under a fine head of determined
steam.

Arley slowed down as she approached the *Expositor* office, her nerves getting the better of her. But when she saw Charles Randall come out the door and head back to the hotel, she hesitated no longer. Duncan sat at the front desk in his shirtsleeves, bent over a telegram form. Besides publishing the *Expositor,* he also operated the seldom-used telegraph machine. When the bell tinkled and he looked up and saw her, he jumped to his feet, grabbed his jacket, and struggled to insert his arms into it.

"Oh, never mind that, Duncan. I was out in public in my apron yesterday so it's all right for me to see you in your shirtsleeves." She didn't know why, but she wasn't having her usual trouble talking to him. Maybe she just didn't have time for that stuff anymore. "Don't forget the way my boarders look most of the time. I'm more than used to disheveled men."

"Disheveled?" he said. "You think I'm disheveled?"

Her head of steam was diminishing. She put her hand to her mouth. "I didn't mean…you're not in the least…what I meant was…" She sat abruptly in the chair beside the desk and took a deep breath. And then another one, and felt calmer again. "I need to talk to you about something."

"Assuredly." He finished putting on his coat anyway. "What is it?" He sat again.

"Remember that article you wrote about ore? With the stibnite and cassiterite?"

"You remember that article? You remember those ores?"

"Well, yeah. Didn't I just say so? Well, what's more valuable than those? More even than gold and silver and coal?"

He thought for a minute. "These are not classified as ores but they are more valuable. Diamonds. Platinum. Blue jade. Perhaps mercury. The rarest, most valuable thing of all, however, is an elemental metal known as osblindium. It's been utilized in some pieces of jewelry crafted for Russian royalty. It is endowed with a glow, an iridescence that's not possible to duplicate artificially. Its other primary use is in paint and in textiles. Even a small amount can give an unmatchable luster. It's extremely difficult to find, laborious to mine, arduous to work with. And unbelievably expensive which, naturally, makes it highly coveted. Why?"

"Is it possible we could have osblindium here?"

"Osblindium in Grubstake?" He smiled wryly. "Our mines have barely yielded the commonest ores. What makes you think they would contain one of the rarest?"

"Well, they've got *something*. Why else are Charles Randall and Morgan so interested in buying them?"

"Morgan wants to buy them, too?" He scratched his head in puzzlement.

"No. But he and Randall are in cahoots. They're looking for something here—something that makes them want to buy mines. If it's not osblindium, what is it?"

Duncan scratched his head some more. "How do you know this?"

"They told me last night. Duncan, something's not right about what they're up to."

He paced the room's perimeter. "That story about Grubstake as a resort did seem questionable if not completely implausible. So perhaps you're right. Perhaps there is something specific they want. Well, I'm convinced we don't have diamonds. Or platinum or mercury. No evidence of all of those. Or of osblindium, for that matter, though I know that at least some of our miners have tried the old traditional folk tests for it and found nothing. Of course, our miners aren't professionals. Perhaps some of their inability to find valuable substances is because they barely know what they're doing."

"But earlier miners found good strikes. My papa did."

"I suspect they also were amateurs—your father was, correct?—but that the lodes were closer to the surface then, and more accessible. All that has been stripped away now, and what remains is more difficult—if not impossible—to excavate. *If* there is anything at all remaining."

"There's got to be something still in those mines. I know it. That's the only way this scheme of Charles Randall's makes sense."

Duncan was quiet for a moment—and Arley thought she could almost hear the wheels and gears working in his brain. Then he nodded and said, "Your logic is convincing about the mine purchases. But osblindium? I consider it must be something other than that."

Arley jumped to her feet. "Okay! Whatever! So what do we do now?" She was ready to go after Morgan and Charles Randall right then. They could figure out what was in the mines later.

"That which every newspaperman understands to be the scrupulous thing. Tell the truth. The only way for our miners to make an efficacious decision about selling their properties is by possessing all the facts. On occasion one must make a decision before this is feasible, but one should have all that are conceivably available."

Part of the reason Duncan's father had found him such a disappointment was his reluctance to act, his need to always be waiting for yet one more fact. His father operated by the seat of his pants, on instinct and guesswork and luck. He thought Duncan was too unadventurous, too cautious, too squeamish. Apparently, one of the few bad decisions his father ever made was his last one, when he'd gone out into that howling blizzard two years before.

"So you need to write an article," Arley said, "saying that there might be something valuable in our mountains and anybody thinking about selling should consider that their mines might be worth a lot more if they waited to see if the valuable thing is there."

"I would write that only if I could acquire a statement to that effect from Mr. Randall, or from your newly arrived boarder, or from any other recognized expert. But I'd also be obliged to say that their mines will be worth naught if nothing is found."

"But we need to get the word out *now*." Arley almost stamped her foot with frustration. "You won't write anything without the statement?"

"Then it would remain hearsay. Gossip. That is not the purpose of a newspaper."

Well, she couldn't argue with that, no matter how much she wanted to. One of the bunch of things she liked about Duncan was his integrity. His father would have published the article without batting an eye. So much rectitude could drive you crazy but it could also make you want to behave better yourself, at least for a while. How could Lacey possibly be perceptive enough to appreciate him?

Arley sighed gustily, resigned. "If I can get it, will you put out a special edition to let everybody know?"

"Immediately."

"Oh," she remembered. "I saw Charles Randall leaving just as I came in. Is he making flyers for another meeting?"

"No."

Dang! Duncan was preserving that weasel's privacy. High morals could really get in the way of finding things out. Then she remembered the form Duncan had been filling out when she came in.

"Sending a telegram?" she asked.

After a long pause, he said, "Maybe."

Hah! she thought. All those morals made it impossible for him to lie to her.

Reading upside down was something Arley had practiced after Amanda had learned the secrets that way in *Sagebrush Secrets*. Before Duncan could get to his desk and retrieve the telegram form, she saw that it was addressed to Mr. Sidney Lockwood. It said,

"Trouble with Morgan and the miners. Stop. Your presence greatly needed. Stop. Randall."

"I have to go now, Duncan. To see if I can get you that statement. Bye." And she ran out with him looking after her.

⚬⊷⦿⊷⦿⊶⚬

Arley went straight to Wing, who was baking rolls. "How did donuts work?" he asked.

She slumped into a chair. "He loved them. And didn't tell me one thing except that he grew up in a bad orphanage."

"Maybe you need more donuts."

"I had plenty. He just clammed up. Oh—but I did find out that he and Randall don't like each other. And that Randall has a couple of little dogs locked up in the room next to his. And that he's asking Mr. Lockwood to come here to help him do whatever he's trying to do."

"So. Lots of information."

"But none of it makes sense. What are those dogs for?"

"You say dogs are little? Sometimes little dogs go into little places looking for little things."

She sat up straight. "You think they're osblindium hunters?"

·113·

Wing stopped kneading and blinked at her. "What kind hunters?"

"Osblindium. It's some rare ore thing, hard to find, hard to mine, and insanely expensive."

"You think we got that here?"

"I *know* we don't have diamonds or any of the other valuable things I can think of, so osblindium's about all that's left that anybody could want. You think dogs could find it?"

"If they can, I think you got some dogs can help them change their minds."

"What? Orville and Wilbur? They don't know anything about osblindium."

"They know plenty about not working, and getting in troubles."

"But those dogs are always locked up. How—"

"I hear you pretty good at picking locks."

After a silent moment, Arley said, "Bridget's been over to buy bread, right?"

Wing looked inscrutably at her. "You want rolls for dinner tonight?"

--ᐧ⊚ᐧ⦿ᐧ⊚ᐧ--

From Wing's she went to the Spittoon for an early sarsaparilla break with Everdene and Bridget.

"That was pretty exciting upstairs yesterday. Did

you find out anything?" Everdene said from behind the bar as she dried the glasses that Bridget was washing.

"Not much," Arley said, plunking herself down on a barstool. "Morgan works for Lockwood Ltd. His job is to find geology kinds of things that will make Mr. Lockwood rich, like oil and coal. Charles Randall works for Mr. Lockwood, too. He's not buying mines to make a resort. He's buying them for Mr. Lockwood because there's probably something rare and valuable in them." As Everdene opened her mouth Arley held up her hand. "No, I don't know what it is. Maybe osblindium."

"Oz—what?" Bridget asked.

"It's some rare, expensive stuff. Maybe they use dogs to find it. I don't know," she almost wailed. "Nothing I find out makes sense. And now Mr. Lockwood's probably coming to Grubstake to make things even worse."

"Sidney Lockwood's coming here?" Everdene asked. Her drying hand went still.

"I think so. Wait. How do you know his name's Sidney? Do you know him?"

Everdene had a far-off look in her eyes. "I used to. A long time ago." The far-off look was replaced by a look of venom. "And I swore that if I ever saw him again, I'd kill him."

Arley jumped off her barstool. "What!"

Even Bridget took her hands out of the dishwater and grabbed a towel. "You're not serious," she exclaimed.

"I sure was when I swore that," Everdene said. "We'll see how serious I still am when he shows up here."

"What happened?" Arley asked.

Everdene put down her towel and leaned on the bar. "I cannot believe I was ever so stupid, but Sidney Lockwood and I were once young and in love. Love! Hah! And he wanted to marry me. But then he decided I wasn't going to be a good partner for him since he was planning to become a millionaire, by hook or by crook, and I wasn't in favor of the crook part. He meant to find somebody who was."

"Did he?" Bridget asked.

"I have no idea. That's when I packed up and came to Grubstake to make my own way as an honest businesswoman who never had to depend on any man ever again in her lifetime." She made a little sound that could have been a stifled sob or a sigh. "And remembering that is making me feel like killing him all over again."

"So this business about buying the mines for a resort that won't ever happen sounds like something he'd do?" Arley asked.

"It sounds exactly like something he'd do. And be proud of it."

"Okay, then. We need to get prepared. Somehow. I talked to Duncan about putting an article in the paper warning the miners, but he won't do it unless I can get proof in writing about what's going on because he's too honest to publish hearsay and speculation. Which I don't know how to do. But I'm thinking about it."

"Duncan's way too good for the lightweight likes of Lacey Bernaise," Bridget said.

"That's what I say, too," Arley said.

"Love," said Everdene, spitting on a spot on the bar and polishing it with her towel, "has nothing to do with logic. Or with common sense, either, more's the pity."

Well, Arley knew that. Love had been such a mystery, puzzle, and nuisance to her. She loved the mother she'd never known, wasn't sure she loved the father she had known but who had paid her barely any attention, loved Everdene who had practically raised her, and had some confused sort of something going on about Duncan. And she wasn't sure it was considerate to talk about the subject in front of Bridget when her husband-to-be had deserted her before she could even get a look at him.

"I've never had a chance to find out anything about love," Bridget said. "But it didn't hurt my feelings that my mail-order fiancé left. Not at all. Whatever made him skedaddle wasn't about me. Anyway, we might not have liked each other. I do know you can't *make* somebody love you, no matter what you do. And why would you want to if you have to pretend you're somebody you aren't?"

"Can't be done," Everdene said. "I tried. Took me about five minutes to say, 'Forget this.' I'm not changing for any man."

All three of them sighed in unison.

From what Arley could gather, love could be a joy, a torment, and a big pain in the patootie.

They looked up at the sound of footsteps on the stairs. Charles Randall was on his way down, splendid as ever in a fresh shirt, shined shoes, and smooth and fragrant shave. "Good morning, ladies," he said, giving his umbrella a little twirl.

Arley wouldn't look at him. Somebody who wasn't even getting up until eleven wasn't a person she could talk to. But Everdene and Bridget both wished him a good morning. He was, after all, paying for two rooms.

"I'll be going down to the Eat 'n' Run for some breakfast," he said jovially. "Anything special you recommend?"

Everdene shrugged. "Ham and eggs. That's about all they got."

Arley muttered, "Rat poison."

"How's that?" Charles Randall asked.

"Nothing."

They watched him cross the room, go out the door, pop open his umbrella, and stop on the wood sidewalk in front. He lifted his hat and said, "Good morning, ma'am."

A quick glance passed among the three of them and then they were on their feet headed for the front window where they hung back behind the dusty velvet curtain, peeking out at Charles Randall and Lacey.

"Good morning," Lacey said from under her pink and white umbrella, and tried to walk around him.

He moved into her path.

"Excuse me," she said primly, but with the tone of somebody used to getting her own way.

"Excuse *me*," he said, "but I can't let a lovely lady like you pass me by on this beautiful morning." It was gray and drizzly. As usual. And two skinny curs—not Orville and Wilbur, for once—wrestled in the mud in the middle of the deserted street.

Arley looked at Everdene and raised her eyebrows all the way to the top of her forehead. Everdene rolled her eyes and nodded.

"Oh," Lacey said and did that thing with her eyelashes. "Well, it *is* a pretty day, isn't it?"

"And a pretty town. Splendid spot for a resort. I don't believe I saw you the other night at my town meeting. I'm Charles Randall, ma'am. And you are—?"

"Lacey Bernaise." She extended her little lace-gloved hand. "Ever so pleased to meet you."

"I was just on my way to the Eat 'n' Run for some breakfast. Would you like to join me for a cup of tea? I could fill you in on what you missed at the meeting."

"Why, that would be very nice. I was headed to the newspaper with a little article for the next edition. It's about the quilt my mother and I just finished. But that can surely wait." She tucked her hand into the crook of his proffered arm and off they went.

Everdene turned to Arley. "Maybe you don't need to worry about her and Duncan."

"I wasn't worried about it," Arley said indignantly. "Why should I worry? They can do what they want with each other, if they want to do anything. It's fine with me. Who cares what they do? Not me."

Everdene and Bridget just looked at her.

"Well. I guess I better get going now. Bye." And she hurried out, her cheeks pink.

As she clomped down the wooden sidewalk she heard growling coming from the alley. Peering down it she saw Wilbur and Orville muzzle-deep in a pile of garbage spilling from a tipped-over barrel. They were arguing over who should have some particularly disgusting piece of who-knew-what. She rushed into the alley and grabbed Wilbur by the scruff of his neck. "Hey! Stop that, you two! Do you want to get sick?" She grabbed Orville, too, and pulled both muddy, stinking dogs out onto the sidewalk.

As the three of them lurched along she noticed Duncan looking open-mouthed at them through the window of the *Expositor.* She gave him a feeble smile as the dogs suddenly decided they needed to be home and took off at a gallop, yanking Arley almost off her feet.

NINE

ONCE HOME, ARLEY WASN'T about to face a day of
chores—not after that embarrassment with Duncan
and the dogs. She still wasn't speaking to them, and
she certainly wasn't letting them in the house until
they'd stood out in the drizzle long enough to quit reek-
ing of garbage. Anyway, she needed something to make
sense. She wanted answers. Quickly she threw together a few sandwiches and tossed them and the leftover donuts into a flour sack. She was going to deliver
lunch to her boarders. So what if she'd never done it
before?

It was big-headed, she knew, and wrong to boot, for

her to think she could recognize something about the mines that nobody, including Morgan, had. Especially since she'd never even been inside one before and still didn't think she could actually enter one—the very idea made the hair on the back of her neck stand up. But she had to do *something* to protect her Grubs. And she'd never been one to just sit around waiting to see what might happen next.

When the rain stopped, as it usually did around midday, Arley took off on her mule, Anabelle. She tried to pick her way around the mud puddles on the rutted track that wound from the end of town up the side of the mountain, past dripping scrubby bushes and piles of mossy rocks. But there were more mud and puddles than track.

By the time they reached the first mine—Purvis's Midas Mine—Anabelle was caked with mud up to her knees, something she just hated. There were no signs of life, and no sounds from inside, though Burrito, Purvis's mule, was dozing in the clearing. Anabelle startled him awake by nuzzling him amorously in the ear.

Arley tiptoed to the Midas's entrance and stood there, looking into the dark and listening to her heart pound. She couldn't see anything that would make a tycoon want to buy the place. "Yoo hoo," she called softly, and then louder. "You in there, Purvis?"

All that came out of the dark mouth was a stream of warm air. She took a step backward.

"Hey, Purvis!" she yelled louder. "I've got sand-wiches!" If the offer of food didn't bring him out, then nothing would. She peered around, listening.

Still there was silence. Now she was getting wor-ried. Could Morgan have found what he was looking for here and done something to Purvis? How far were these thugs willing to go to get what they wanted? She was picturing poor confused little Purvis lying some-where in a pool of his own—

"Hey, Arley," he said, appearing out of the dark at the mouth of the mine, his hands full of papers. "What are you doing here?"

Her legs were so watery she had to sit down on a nearby boulder. "Where *were* you?" she said crossly. "Didn't you hear me calling?"

His forehead puckered. "Are you mad at me? I guess I was concentrating so hard I didn't hear you." He hung his head in contrition.

"No, no, it's okay," she said, guilty and remorseful. "I just wanted to bring you some lunch."

"You already made me lunch." He pointed to a

tin bucket just inside the mine entrance. "Like you always do. Did I forget something?" His forehead puckered again.

She forced a laugh. "I guess *I* forgot I'd made it. Well, here, have another one. Two's better than one, right? What are all those papers?"

He looked at the pile in his hand. "Oh, these? These are some of my favorite parchments. I keep them in a box in the Midas so they'll be safe. Sometimes it seems like somebody's been going through the stuff in my room. I know these are so beautiful somebody'd want to take them. So I come up here when I want to look at them." He looked shyly at her. "Would you like to see them? You don't have to if you don't want to."

"I'd love to," Arley said, silently vowing to never again rummage through anything in Purvis's room.

One by one, he handed her pieces of parchment decorated around the edges with beautifully colored pictures of scenes from Grubstake, making the mud, the mules, the dogs, the ramshackle buildings, and the mountains look somehow enchanted.

"Is this how you see Grubstake?" Arley asked.

"Well, sure. I know it's not perfect here, but all these pictures are things I really saw. I like the way they look."

"I do, too," she said, pretty sure Charles Randall wasn't looking at Grubstake through such kind eyes.

On each parchment were words so seriously misspelled that Arley had to struggle to make them out.

Plan ahed or therz trubble at the frunt door.

Beter to bee a lyon fur a dai then a sheeep all yur lif.

Receepee for suckcess—rize erly, werk late, strik ozblindium.

Reading that last one, Arley almost dropped the parchment.

"Purvis, these are great. I can see why you want to keep them safe." As if just noticing it, she said, "This one here, the recipe for success—does that say, 'Strike osblindium'?"

"Yeah. That's a good saying, right?"

"A very good saying. So, ah, where did you hear about that...what is it...osblindium?"

"Well, we usually call it by its nickname, but all miners know about it. It's sort of like the Holy Grail of mining. Everybody looks for it, nobody ever finds it. Except in Russia, I guess."

"Any chance we have some around here?"

He laughed, and then got serious. "Have you heard that?"

"Have *you*?"

"No. But it would be nice, wouldn't it? And I've tried to find it, too. I rubbed tobacco on the places I thought it could be—that's supposed to react to it somehow—I just don't know how. And I didn't smoke the leftovers, or chew them either, Arley, I promise. I even brought Orville and Wilbur up here once to help me look for it, because once I read that dogs can sniff it out. But they must be some other kind of dogs. Wilbur and Orville just ran around, and ate my lunch, and chased a marmot. They were useless."

"They usually are." Between the dogs and the to-bacco, osblindium didn't seem quite such an unlikely possibility anymore as the thing Morgan, Charles Randall, and Mr. Lockwood were expecting to find in Grub-stake's mines.

"You want to come see my mine?" Purvis asked. "I know it's not much now, but once it had a lot of hope in it. And you've never come up here before."

Arley stood up. "I'm...I'm sure it's just wonderful. But you know how I am about going in the mines. I can get close, but..." She shook her head. "Sorry. I'm just a big chicken, that's all. But maybe someday, okay? I'm going over to the Powder Room—I mean, the Powder Keg—to see Outdoor John. He needs a donut, too, I think."

"Okay. See you later. Thanks for the extra lunch. And, um, could you leave me another donut?"

⸺◦⸺◉⸺◉⸺◦⸺

As Arley and Anabelle made their way past the tumbled rocks and damp underbrush toward Outdoor John's mine, Arley wondered for the thousandth time why he'd named it the Powder Keg. Those were things that blew up. Admittedly, it was a very tough and manly name, but surely the Abundant and Stable would have been a more optimistic choice.

She found him sitting outside with a pile of rocks beside him, and who should he be showing them to but Morgan.

"Don't!" Arley yelled as she came riding up to them. "Don't show him those rocks!"

Millicent, grazing in the gorse, jumped and Outdoor John looked up, suddenly anxious. "Why? What's wrong with them? And what are you doing here, Arley? Is something the matter? You never come up here."

"I just...I'm bringing you lunch. You know. How I do that." She dismounted from Anabelle with her sack. Anabelle moseyed over to Mrs. Jones, Outdoor John's mule, for a little girl talk.

With a puzzled look Outdoor John held up his lunch bucket. "You always pack our lunches. In the morning. I already ate mine." He brightened. "But I can always eat some more. What is it?"

"Sandwiches. And, uh, donuts." She'd avoided looking directly at Morgan until then. He tipped his big black hat in her direction and didn't say a word. But he kept his eyes on the bag with the donuts.

Outdoor John took the sandwich Arley handed him, and said, "How come I shouldn't show him these rocks? He doesn't need me to point them out. They're lying all over the place. These aren't anything special anyway. They're just ones I thought were pretty."

"I'm admiring them," Morgan said. "Very nice."

Of course he'd understand exactly what he was looking at. He had all kinds of books about rocks. But he wasn't supposed to know she knew that.

"Uh, how come you want to look at rocks?" she asked, handing him a donut. He looked at it for a long moment and finally took it. But he didn't chomp right into it the way Outdoor John had. He held it, looked at it, even seemed to be smelling it.

"Rocks?" she reminded him.

"I like rocks," he said, reluctantly looking up at her from the donut. "They're interesting. They stay put. You can count on them. They don't talk back. They're predictable."

"You sound like you like rocks better than people."

"Most rocks. Most people."

"You mean there are rocks you don't like?"

"Limestone—too porous. Sandstone—too crumbly. Basalt—too sharp. Osblin—" He stopped.

"Osblin?" she asked innocently.

"Rocks don't ask so many questions, either." He took a bite of the donut.

"So why didn't you want me to show him the rocks?" Outdoor John asked again.

"Never mind," Arley said. "Say, did you know we're going to have a very important visitor in Grubstake soon?"

"Who?" Outdoor John asked.

"A big shot by the name of Mr. Sidney Lockwood."

Morgan dropped his donut, but caught it before it hit the ground. It pleased Arley to see that she knew something he didn't. Obviously Charles Randall hadn't told him of this plan. Maybe they weren't in such cahoots as she'd thought.

"Never heard of him," Outdoor John said. "Who is he?"

"To tell you the truth, I never heard of him either. But Wing says he's a big tycoon with his fingers—probably his whole hand—in a lot of rich pies. He even helped build our railroad. And it seems that he's the one wanting to make a resort out of Grubstake. He's supplying the money to buy the mines. Right, Morgan?"

"Who told you this?"

"Charles Randall sent a telegram this morning asking him to come. You think he will?" Oh, she was enjoying this.

Without a word, he stuffed the donut into his mouth, leaped into the saddle, and he and Millicent took off down the mountain.

Arley noted there was a plug of tobacco left on the rock where he had been sitting.

"Is it yours?" she asked Outdoor John, giving him a stern look. "You know the rules."

He held his hand up, palms facing her. "Not mine. Nope. Not at all. Must be his." He got a sly glint in his eye. "But if you give it to me, I can return it to him."

"Have you ever seen him chewing?" She hung on to the plug, holding it gingerly, with her thumb and forefinger.

Outdoor John scratched his head. "Can't say I have. And he should have offered me a chaw if that's his. That's the etiquette, you know. Always share your plug."

"There's tobacco etiquette?" Arley asked.

"Why, sure. Don't spit on each other's boots. Don't

spit into the wind. Don't spit on the floor. Don't spit in bed. Things like that."

"How about just not spitting at all?"

"You mean swallow it? Oh, Arley, I don't think that would be a good idea."

"No, I don't mean swallow it," she said exasperated. "I mean don't chew it at all."

"Well, we pretty much don't. It's expensive, and we can't afford it. So it's a real treat when—I mean—"

"I know what you mean. So if Morgan wasn't chewing it, or sharing it, what do you think he was doing with it?"

"How should I know? The only other thing I know you can do with tobacco is test for pay dirt, and everybody here's already done that long ago. The first thing you learn about mining, as a beginner, is to look for the most expensive stuff first."

"I thought the most expensive stuff was something called osblindium."

"Yeah. That's right."

"But you said you looked for pay dirt."

"Osblindium *is* pay dirt. Osblindium is just too big a mouthful."

"You mean, all this time when I heard you guys talking about pay dirt, you really meant pay dirt?"

"Uh, yeah. Isn't that what I just said?"

"Osblindium is pay dirt?" Arley wanted to make sure she had this right.

"Yes! I keep telling you that. You know, you're starting to remind me of Purvis."

"And you all knew about how to test for it? How come I've never even heard of it until today? How come nobody ever told me about it?"

"Huh. I guess we figured your papa had. All miners know about it. But why should we talk about something we don't have?"

"Are we sure we don't have it?"

"Well, nobody's ever found any. Course it's beyond rare and wicked hard to locate, too. And it's true none of us is any kind of expert. Mostly we're just plain old diggers, but we do look for everything—coal, diamonds, anything that'll make us a buck. We got a whole list of things that aren't here. And pay dirt is right up there at the top."

The rain started again then, the way it always seemed to do in the afternoon. "Uh-oh," Outdoor John said. "You want to go inside the mine? It's dry in there and safe from the lightning. And you should see what Morgan brought me. A muskrat *and* a porcupine. The muskrat's pretty fresh. The porcupine—well, I can fix him up. All those quills can cover up a lot of decomposition."

"That's...that's great. I wish I could go inside with you. I'm sure it's real nice. But you know me and mines. I'd better get off the mountain, away from the lightning, now. And I'm sure I'll get to see the, uh, the deceased later."

As she and Anabelle plodded back down the mountain in the rain, occasionally skidding on the steep, muddy path, jumping at every thunderclap, she thought about Outdoor John's room, full of pelts and wire forms looking like silver skeletons, bottles of Duck Degreaser and Snout Polish, and a bucket of glass eyeballs that seemed to follow her everywhere when she was in there. No snooping in Outdoor John's room, that was for sure. Not with all those eyes watching her.

Arley considered the stuffed marmot he'd given her for her birthday. It was so lifelike it gave her the willies every single time she opened the door of her room and saw it sitting there on the windowsill as if it had just climbed in. Maybe he *would* be better off with a career of stuffing and mounting instead of mining. Maybe there wasn't anything valuable in his mine, and he *should* sell while the selling was good. Who was she to be telling her miners what to do? What did she know? All she had were a bunch of suspicious suspicions and not one solid fact. Maybe she ought to be telling her boarders to sell for the biggest price they could squeeze out of Charles Randall and go have normal lives someplace else.

She felt a sudden pang at how much she would miss that bucket of eyeballs. And the misspelled notes. And the little wax gnomes with the wicks sticking out of their heads.

"I hate it when I get confused," she muttered. "I like my mind to stay made up, like my bed! Oooh, I wish I knew for sure what Morgan is looking for, and whether we really have it."

—◦⟨◉⟩•⟨◉⟩◦—

Once home, after drying Anabelle off and giving her a carrot to soothe her rumpled vanity, which smarted from having to trot through town soaking wet and dirty, Arley found the weekly edition of the *Expositor* on her front porch. Mickey from the livery had so little to do that he doubled as Grubstake's paper boy once a week. She scooped it up and dropped it onto the hall table. She knew plenty about the recent happenings in Grubstake and the adventures of Orville and Wilbur. Right now she had to get into some dry clothes, put some salted beef to soak so it would be ready to mix with the beans for supper, and scrub the kitchen floor.

She finished scrubbing as it continued to rain hard, guaranteeing muddy footprints no matter how much she got after her boarders about taking off their boots. It was starting to look as if spring were going to skip Grubstake this year. And maybe summer, too. She built a fire in the parlor and sat down with the *Expositor*. In large screaming letters, so completely unlike Duncan that she knew he was excited about having some real big news for once, the headline read **SIDNEY LOCKWOOD COMING TO GRUBSTAKE**.

The article went on to state that a telegram had been received that morning saying Mr. Lockwood was on the way to inspect his future resort and to meet the mine owners who would benefit from his largesse. He would also be offering bonuses to encourage sales.

Arley realized that Lockwood had reacted immediately to Charles Randall's telegram. That didn't seem good. Her visit to Duncan's office that morning when she had learned about the telegram now seemed a long time ago considering all that had happened since. But it also seemed like a short time for an important person with a packed schedule to make a decision.

Whatever he was worried about must be serious, she thought, *to get him to leave his luxurious city offices to come stay at the Spittoon Saloon and Hotel.*

Because she believed that action was always better than inaction, she jumped to her feet, ready. But for what? She made a little whimpering noise and walked around the parlor wringing her hands. "Think," she muttered. *"Think!"*

Okay. Who knew what was going on better than anybody? Not Morgan. He didn't know about Lockwood's visit, and he wouldn't talk anyway. So Charles Randall was it. He knew everything, and he was so smug he might trip over his own ego and tell her something.

She grabbed her wet shawl and went back out into the rain and cold. She sprinted across the street, jumped up onto the wooden sidewalk, stamped ten percent of the mud off her boots, and hustled into the Spittoon.

Charles Randall was sitting at a table with the *Expositor* and a cup of tea. Arley gave him a curt nod and sat down across the table from him.

"Won't you join me?" he asked dryly.

"Okay," she said, wondering where Everdene had gotten the tea. She'd never seen anybody drink tea in the Spittoon. "Anything good in the paper?"

"Your editor—Duncan McKenzie, I believe—does quite an excellent job with so little material. I can see why his stories, which the residents have told me about, are so popular. Such a happy ending this one has, with the vein of gold going through only the mines of the good guys. Too bad that's not how it happens in real life."

Arley was a little discouraged with real life herself

at the moment. In one of her Penny Dreadfuls, nothing would have been this frustrating.

"I see your boss is coming to town," she said.

Charles Randall sipped his tea. "Yes, Mr. Lockwood is the figure behind this resort plan. He often prefers to remain anonymous so as not to influence transactions. I'm sure I could convince him to make it worth your while if you helped persuade the rest of these miners to sell. A special bonus added to the price of your own mine. A nice fat bonus. Think of what pretty things you could buy with that. Somewhere besides Grubstake."

She tried to think about pretty things. But all that came to her mind were Purvis's parchments, and Prairie Martin's gnomes, and Outdoor John's bright-eyed menagerie. Then she thought about dimity and ribbons and parasols.

"Feh." The sound came out involuntarily.

"What?" Randall asked.

"I was coughing," she said, and gave a couple of little hacks for proof.

"Well? What do you think about that offer?"

"I don't see how I could persuade anybody to sell when I don't think they know enough about why you want their mines. And *I'm* definitely not ready to sell. But maybe you could persuade me if I had more information."

He leaned back in his chair and took a sip of his tea. "What do you want to know?"

Whoa. She hadn't expected cooperation. And she doubted that's what she was actually getting. Charles Randall was too tricky for that. But she wasn't going to let any opportunity for information go to waste. "How come you're buying mines and not the hotel, say, or the Opera House? Wouldn't you want those for your resort?"

"Ah. Well, we're trying to find the owner of the Opera House, who apparently left town rather suddenly for parts unknown when his fortunes failed. And I've spoken to Miss Hannigan about the hotel, but so far we've not been able to agree on terms." He smiled smugly.

"You've talked to Everdene about the hotel?" Arley asked, shocked.

"Yes. I understood she wanted to keep our discussions private." He got smugger still.

Arley couldn't believe him. Could she? Was what she had always feared about to happen? Would Everdene really disappear from her life the way everybody else had, or might be about to? She felt suddenly cold and alone. But she'd have to think about all this later. Right now she had a mission.

"Okay, then, why are the mines so important? What do they have to do with a resort?"

"They would be such a quaint attraction for our resort guests. An adventure. To have a tour of a real mine. To hold a pickaxe, to pat a mule, to—well, whatever else you do in a mine. This resort would be unique, offering a mining experience."

Arley, whose whole life had been connected with mining experiences, didn't see the allure. But maybe he was right. Maybe it was there.

"Then what's Morgan for? Why is he looking in the mines?" She couldn't reveal she'd heard him say he hadn't found what he was looking for since she'd gotten that knowledge by eavesdropping.

"Morgan is our mine inspector. He has to make sure all the mines we buy are safe for the guests to be in. He makes an inventory of what needs to be done to bring them up to our highest standards of safety. He's looking for major problems—and it's always a relief when he says he hasn't found any."

"And the dogs—Muggs and Brute?"

"I told you. They're my beloved pets. I never go anywhere without them."

"So beloved you keep them locked in a room away from you?"

"Just so I can get some rest and some work done. They're so devoted to me that they always try to get in my lap when we're together." After a long pause, while he kept his eyes on her, he said, "Any more questions?"

For once in her life, she didn't have a one—because she had the feeling that whatever she asked him, he'd have an answer for. And as confused as she was just then, it was possible that some of what he was telling her might even be true.

"When's Mr. Lockwood coming? The next train's not for a few weeks, you know."

"Mr. Lockwood doesn't worry about the things regular people have to think about. He has his own private railway car and engine. He can come and go any time he likes. He'll be arriving day after tomorrow. Then I think you'll see some real changes around here. He always gets what he wants."

"Really?" Her voice came out in a sort of squeak. The last time she'd felt this same sense of foreboding was the day two years ago when she was in the garden digging up some potatoes and heard an explosion from the direction of the Never Mine. She hoped she wasn't about to experience that sense again.

He patted his mouth with his handkerchief. "Now please excuse me. I have some things to do to get ready for Mr. Lockwood's visit." He went up the stairs rather jauntily.

Arley sat looking into the dregs of Charles Randall's teacup, her chin in her hand. *Was* she on the wrong track? What was so great about Grubstake anyway, that she should be working so hard to hang on to? Why shouldn't they all just get out and leave whatever was or wasn't in the mines behind? Just because she'd lived there all her life didn't mean anything—there *had* to be nicer places. Maybe she'd even get a chance to see London or Denver. Besides, if Everdene left, what was there to stay for?

Everdene came out of her room behind the Spittoon with one of her blood-and-thunder Penny Dreadfuls in her hand. "Oh. Hi, Arley. Is it sarsaparilla time? I've been rereading some of my bloodiest ones, getting ready to see Sidney Lockwood again."

"Everdene," Arley said, looking up at her. "Have you been talking to Charles Randall about selling the hotel?"

Everdene looked startled for a moment and then sat down across from Arley. She took both of Arley's hands and looked her straight in the eye. "I was going to tell you. Because this town is dying. I think we both know that. Maybe it's already dead. The two of us, we're businesswomen. And to be that, we need businesses. How do you think I can hang on here if the miners clear out? What if your boarders sell and leave?

And whatever Sidney Lockwood may have planned for Grubstake, I don't want to stick around to see. Do you?"

"You know I don't. But, Everdene, why didn't you tell me? If I'd known *everybody* was going to leave, I'd have quit trying so hard to find out what was happening."

"Would you? Or would you have kept trying even while you were packing up to leave?"

Arley shrugged. "I don't know. I guess I would. Even if I was leaving, I'd still want to know why."

"So you *can* keep trying to know. No matter how we end up."

Arley stood, withdrawing her hand's from Everdene's. "I think I'll skip the sarsaparilla today."

With her hand on the doorknob, she turned back to Everdene. "Did you know that the miners call osblindium pay dirt?"

"They do? That's what they mean when they say they can never strike pay dirt?"

"That's it. Seems like Grubstake is all dirt and no pay."

She went out into the downpour.

TEN

WHEN ARLEY GOT HOME, she lay down on the hearth
rug in front of the fire between the two sleeping dogs.
Where would the three of them ever have a cozy home
like this again? Where would there ever be a place that
the dogs could run freely and safely, where everybody
would know them and understand them (even if they
didn't approve of them)? She sat up. Moping helped
nothing. She had to *act*.

When she stood, the dogs moved closer together, replacing her warmth with each other's. She went up the
stairs and into her bedroom, where she took Bridget's
long hairpin from her bureau drawer. She didn't know

where Morgan was, but if he hadn't returned by now he must be holed up somewhere dry, waiting for the rain to stop. And if he came back and caught her— well, she'd deal with that then. She brought the fireplace poker with her just in case.

Efficiently, she picked the lock on the door to Morgan's room and went directly to the bottom drawer. Inside were all the papers she remembered from her first exploration, as well as a few new ones on top of the pile.

She picked up the new pages and read them. They were reports for Mr. Lockwood from Morgan about the mines, and they weren't about safety hazards either. They were about osblindium. Except that he hadn't found any yet. But he said he knew it was there. All the signs indicated that. He said he could almost smell it, all he had to do was locate it. He was frustrated, too, but he knew that with just a little more time, he could find it.

She jumped up and down. This was just what she needed! Duncan would have to print his special edition now! They could warn the Grubs! They could thwart Mr. Lockwood and save Grubstake. Later she could worry about how they could find the osblindium by themselves, how they could mine it, and how they could survive until they solved these problems.

Arley stuffed the most recent report inside her dress, relocked the door, transferred the report to beneath her mattress, and went downstairs again.

—◦·◎·◦·◉·◦◦—

Supper was an awkward affair. Prairie Martin was quite pushed out of shape that Arley hadn't come to see him at his mine (which had no name because he never had been able to decide what to call it) when she'd visited Outdoor John and Purvis at theirs. With sandwiches and donuts, which he *never* got enough of. He understood about the lightning, but he still felt left out and sulky. Only after she promised to bring him fresh donuts from Wing's the very next day did he stop complaining, though not pouting.

Morgan was totally silent and appeared to be thinking hard about something, which Arley surmised was *Where is that darn osblindium?*

After supper Outdoor John practically ran upstairs to get started on his muskrat and porcupine. Morgan also went to his room, and Prairie Martin hung around the fire for a while muttering about donuts until he, too, went off to bed.

When only Purvis was left, Arley grabbed his arm and whispered, "I need you to do something for me. Something very, very secret. Can you keep a secret?"

"Is it a very serious secret?" he asked, peering at her with a worried look.

"The most serious kind of secret there is," she said, bracing herself for a lot of long explaining.

He surprised her by not needing any. "If you say so, then I know it's true. And I'll do whatever you want me to. I don't need to know why."

To her astonishment, tears filmed her eyes. That he trusted her enough not to need an explanation was the best compliment he could have given her. And the prospect maybe of someday soon not having Purvis to explain things to anymore made her blink more tears away.

"Are you all right, Arley?" Purvis asked. "Did I say something wrong?"

"No, you're fine. I'm fine. Come on."

She took him upstairs and into her bedroom. She brought Morgan's report out from under her mattress and said, "Can you copy this? Exactly?"

He studied it for a minute. "Sure," he said. "But I'm not positive all these words are spelled right. You want me to copy them the way they are, or spell them better?"

"Just the way they are, even if they look wrong. Can you do it tonight?"

"You don't want any pictures around the edges?

Because that's what takes the time. The printing, that's fast."

"Just the words. No pictures, okay?"

"Okay. I know you'll tell me someday what it was for."

"I'll tell you tomorrow. You're doing a very good thing, Purvis. I promise."

"I'll stay up all night if I have to. You'll have it first thing in the morning, I promise." He went solemnly down the hall to his room.

—◦⊙∙◉∙⊙◦—

The next morning it was still raining hard, so Arley's boarders decided to stay home from their mines and have a day off. Digging around in the dark had proved to be fruitless anyway, and if they might soon be selling, well, it just didn't seem so important to ride a wet mule up to spend the day at a worthless hole in the ground. This would be a good day for some five card stud in front of the stove.

Morgan, apparently made of sterner stuff, had ridden off on Millicent in the rain up toward the mines. *No doubt doing more safety checks,* Arley thought dryly.

True to his word, Purvis had delivered the copy of Morgan's report—duplicated exactly, down to the letterhead—to Arley before breakfast. She sneaked the original report back into Morgan's drawer, tucked Purvis's copy inside the bodice of her dress, and had an extra cup of coffee to fortify herself for the dash to the *Expositor.* While she drank it she considered that stubbornness was a character trait with nothing to recommend it. All it did was make trouble for the character who had it. But there she was, stuck with it, so there was no avoiding going out in the dang rain.

Arley cast a glance at her boarders settled around the kitchen table with their cards and their crumbly snacks, and at the dogs underneath the table, waiting for the crumbs—a sight she could no longer take for granted and be annoyed about. She sighed, cussed her stubbornness one more time, and left the warm and cozy kitchen for a walk in the cold rain.

She rushed breathlessly into the *Expositor* office where Duncan sat at his desk looking out the window. "Hello, Arley," he said, not changing his gaze. "Lousy day, huh?"

"Why, yes," she said, wondering where his fancy vocabulary had gone. "Something wrong?"

"It's raining."

"That's true. Nothing new there, though."

"There's hardly ever anything new around here. And when there is, it's bad."

"I think the weather is getting you down," Arley

said. "Maybe I've got something that'll cheer you up. Something you've been waiting for."

He finally turned in her direction. "What?"

"You know that proof you wanted? About what might be in the mines? I've got it."

He stood up. "You do?" He sounded dubious. "Let's see."

"Just a minute." She turned her back while she struggled to extract Morgan's report from her damp bodice. It reminded her of the way she'd struggled with her knife the first time she'd seen Morgan. She hoped this struggle would be more necessary and less embarrassing.

Duncan unfolded the paper, which had survived the trip in good shape, and read it. He looked up at her, then read it again. "Where did you acquire this?"

"Purvis copied it *exactly* from a report Morgan wrote. See? He signed it. It's the real thing. I guarantee it. You can keep it. I put the original back so Morgan never missed it."

He studied it for a moment longer. "So we really could have osblindium," he mused. "A few years ago this would have been the answer to many prayers. Now it may be too late. Once people perceive that they can depart, and be paid handsomely to do so, it's difficult to change their thinking. And when the Bernaises, who have greatly enjoyed their elevated status here, consider going elsewhere, I think the balance is tipped." He shook his head dejectedly. "But I'll publish it. I just can't promise it'll make any difference."

"The Bernaises are leaving? I thought Mrs. Bernaise needed to be here for her health." That news didn't bother Arley the way it seemed to be affecting Duncan. Or maybe that's not what was making him so gloomy. But something sure was.

"According to Lacey, she's cured. And Lacey appears to have some quite grand plans of her own." He cast a glance across the street to the Eat 'n' Run.

"With Charles Randall, you mean?" Arley was still trying to figure out what was actually tipping.

"That seems to be the case. They were walking together this morning under a large umbrella. Lacey— who hesitates to leave the house when any sort of weather even threatens—was out in a downpour."

"You'll miss her? Or her mother's cooking? Or...or what?"

"I think—" He sounded a little sheepish. "Well, now that you mention the cooking.... but mostly what I'm seeing is how Grubstake is shrinking. So fast. I've lived here all my life."

"I know." They were quiet together, remembering and stewing. It was enough to make anybody gloomy.

Duncan cleared his throat. "Well. I shall print this as a special broadsheet edition of the *Expositor* and distribute it to the few souls who remain undecided— if there are any."

"Okay." She waited a minute to see if he was going to say anything else, but he just began setting type, so she opened the door. "Bye."

"Good-bye," he said, not looking up.

Arley stood out on the wooden sidewalk wishing someone would come along with a huge umbrella for her. But no one did, so she set off into the downpour. As she passed the Eat 'n' Run, wet and bedraggled, fluffy pink Lacey emerged with Charles Randall holding the giant umbrella over her.

"Why, Arley," she said. "Look at you. Such weather we're having." She gave Charles Randall a twinkly smile.

"Just perfect for a resort, apparently," Arley retorted.

Charles Randall chuckled.

"Well, obviously you like it," Lacey said, "since I hear you're not willing to sell your mine. The one you're too cowardly to go into."

Arley stood, dripping, mouth open, staring at Lacey. They'd never been friends, that was certainly true, but this open warfare was new. Was it because Lacey'd be leaving soon and wouldn't have to live with whatever she started?

When Arley said nothing, Lacey went on. "But come to think about it, I believe Grubstake *is* the perfect place for you. It always has been. This is the deadest dead end there is for all those who have nowhere else to go. Fortunately, I do."

Arley's mind was a tornado of responses ranging from tears to a desire to commit homicide. She couldn't decide which was more appropriate. So once more she was silent.

"My dear," Charles Randall said to Lacey. "I believe you've made her speechless. Which I'm quite enjoying. But perhaps you've been a bit unkind."

"One thing I always do is tell the truth. You can't imagine what it's been like living here with no one of my caliber to associate with."

Caliber. That made Arley think about guns, not companions—and once again she had homicide on her mind.

"Perhaps we should let her go on her way," Charles Randall said. "She's looking rather, um, disarranged. But remember, Miss Pickett, my offer to buy your properties still stands. Then perhaps you can move to a more, um, compatible location."

Lacey wiggled her fingers at Arley. "Ta ta." And she went off under the umbrella with that rat, Charles Randall.

Arley's fury rooted her to the sidewalk until they had disappeared in the sheets of rain. Then she rushed into the Spittoon, so beside herself she was practically foaming at the mouth, the way the dogs had been.

"Jumping juniper!" Everdene exclaimed when she saw her. "What happened to you?"

For a moment all Arley could do was to make incoherent sounds. Everdene came and put her arms around her. "What *is* it, Lemon Drop?"

"Lacey!" she finally sputtered.

"Oh, Lacey," Everdene said. "She never changes."

"Oh, yes, she has," Arley said. "She's hooked up with Charles Randall and she's really turned herself loose. I won't even repeat what she said to me."

"Forget it," Everdene said, giving her a hug and squeezing out enough water to make a puddle on the floor. "You're worth ten of her."

Arley wasn't feeling like even one of herself just then. "I don't know about that. But maybe you're right about Grubstake. Maybe it *is* finished and we should just give up and save ourselves a lot of trouble."

Everdene got some towels from behind the bar and began mopping Arley. "Not until I get my crack at Sidney Lockwood. Then we'll talk."

"You won't have to wait long. He's coming tomorrow."

"Good. My derringer is loaded."

—◦◦⊚◦,◦⊚◦◦—

Arley spent the rest of that rainy day in her room with *Rustler's Rhapsody* which, for the first time, seemed pretty tame compared to what was happening in real life.

ELEVEN

THE NEXT MORNING, as if in honor of Mr. Lockwood, the rain stopped and a misty sunshine appeared. But once again nobody went to the mines—except for Morgan, who got up early, made his own breakfast, and took off on Millicent right after. The others were going to be at the station when that train arrived, even if they had to wait all day. Mickey from the livery had been commissioned by Charles Randall to bring Grubstake's only real carriage—a battered, weather-beaten contraption pulled by a sleepy old piebald. Both Mickey and the horse dozed as they waited.

Duncan had come to the station, too, and while he waited he passed out his special edition of the *Exposi-*

tor forewarning the miners of Mr. Lockwood's actual objective. There was murmuring among the miners as they read the article, and then the discarded *Expositors* accumulated on the ground and the Grubs went back to waiting and speculating about how they would spend their new riches.

Prairie Martin went around with his copy of the *Expositor* asking, "How can you sell when there could be pay dirt in your mines and then they'd be worth a lot more?"

"I'm sick of waiting for things that never happen," George the Hermit said. "Even if I have pay dirt, do you know how long it would be before that stuff could be mined? I want to have some fun sooner than that."

Shouts of agreement rose around him.

Prairie Martin could only shake his head in amazement—all those decisions made so quickly! While his head was filled up with *Sell? Don't sell? Osblindium? No osblindium? Leave? Stay?*

Duncan just sat on the station bench staring at the ground between his knees, watching his special edition of the *Expositor* get trampled into the waterlogged ground.

It was mid-afternoon before the chug of the engine could be heard coming up the mountain track. By the time the train pulled into the station almost every

Grub was standing on tiptoe, waiting. Every Grub except Everdene, Arley, and Bridget, who were back at the hotel, waiting. Everdene had refused to go to Sidney Lockwood—he would have to come to her—and Arley and Bridget were giving her moral support. But Arley felt as if she too were on tiptoe. Bridget sat playing solitaire at a table and Everdene paced behind the bar while her little pearl-handled derringer lay on top.

They heard the entourage coming before they saw it—boots on the wooden sidewalk, a horse's hooves sucking out of the mud, the clatter and jingle of bridles, and the loud excited voices of the Grubs. It all came to a halt in front of the Spittoon.

Bridget got to her feet, shoving the deck of cards into the pocket of her clean apron. Everdene stopped pacing and clutched the edge of the bar so hard her knuckles went white. And Arley lurked at the side of the door, peering out through the window.

The carriage door, loose on its hinges, fell open and a man stepped out. His face was unlined though his hair and mustache were an elegant silver color, and so well barbered they seemed to have been trimmed with surveying tools. He looked fit and was exquisitely dressed, all highly polished boots and knife creases. There was no other way to put it: He was as handsome as a Penny Dreadful hero. Arley could see why Everdene had fallen for him when she was young and stupid.

He walked with a commanding gait through the doors of the Spittoon and stood just inside them looking around while everyone else stacked up behind him. His gaze passed quickly over Arley, rested for an instant on Bridget, skimmed the rough floor, the old tables and chairs, paused at the polished bar and the gun, lifted to Everdene, stopped, and held.

For a long moment they looked into each other's eyes. Mr. Lockwood finally said, in a voice filled with astonishment, "Everdene? Everdene Hannigan?"

She nodded.

"Do you remember me?" he asked.

"Were you hoping I'd forget you?"

His eyes went to the derringer.

"I see you remember what I told you the last time I saw you," she said.

He smiled a confident smile. "A lot of people have said that to me. And I'm still here." He threw his arms out wide.

She picked up the gun, and the crowd around the doorway gasped.

"I'm a very good shot," Everdene said. "I've been practicing. Waiting for you."

Mr. Lockwood dropped his arms. "Heh, heh," he said uneasily. "I don't think your sheriff would like that."

"Grubstake has no sheriff," she said, not lowering the gun. "We make up our own rules around here. And none of us likes being taken advantage of."

"Oh, now, Everdene," he said, holding out his hands to her. "I'm trying to give you an opportunity. One it appears you sorely need."

She cocked the pistol and as she did so, a burly bald man with a fancy waxed mustache charged across the room and tweaked the derringer out of her hand as if it were a toy.

"Thank you, Archie," Mr. Lockwood said as Everdene rubbed her wrist and the crowd exhaled the breath they'd been holding. "Archie takes care of things for me. He'll be staying here, overseeing things in town. I'll be sleeping on my train with my cook and my guard dog. It's been trained to kill to protect me, so don't anybody get any ideas." He glared at Everdene. "Now, we're going to inspect this resort-in-waiting and then we'll be back for a drink. Who's this?" He pointed at Bridget.

"I'm Bridget," she said. "I work here."

"I bet you'd like to be working somewhere else, wouldn't you?"

"I like it just fine here," she said, meeting his eyes.

"Hmmm," he said. "And who's this?" He pointed at Arley.

"Arley Pickett," she said.

"Ah, yes. The troublemaker." He examined her through narrowed eyes. "You don't look like much to worry about."

"That's how much you know," she said, realizing that Charles Randall must have been sending Mr. Lockwood other telegrams describing the Grubs. She decided that she'd die before she'd sell her mine—or anything else—to him, even if it never produced another gram of anything.

He laughed in her face. Turning to Charles Randall, who stood behind him, he said, "Where's Morgan? I didn't see him at the train."

Randall shrugged. "Up at the mines, I hear. He took the dogs."

"Well, that's something, isn't it? A good sign." Mr. Lockwood clapped his hands. "Archie, get your gear up to your room and then we'll take a walk around." He pointed a finger behind the counter. "Everdenc, you and I will talk later."

"Shoot first, talk later, you mean," she said, still rubbing her wrist.

Except for one muffled chuckle, the crowd of Grubs was remarkably quiet. Arley couldn't figure out if they were intimidated by Sidney Lockwood, or afraid Everdene would be provoked into killing him before they could sell him their mines, but they were keeping their mouths shut.

Once Bridget had escorted Archie to his room where he deposited his things, Mr. Lockwood set out to walk up and down the town, poking into every building, inhabited or not. The miners followed him, curious about the man who could transform their lives. Even Lacey Bernaise was in the crowd, Fifi tucked under her arm, taking a good look at her first tycoon.

Arley and Bridget stayed behind with Everdene, who looked a bit shaken.

"Never mind Archie," Arley said. "He's just a big dumb ape."

"That's the worst kind of ape," said Everdene. "They follow orders blindly."

"She's right," Bridget said. "I've seen that kind before. He's more dangerous than Mr. Lockwood *or* Charles Randall."

"Great," Everdene said. "The last thing in the world I want to do is to sell out to that...that...reptile. But it looks like I'm not going to have a choice." She reached under the bar for the sarsaparilla jug and poured herself a stiff one.

Bridget laid out another hand of solitaire. "We're

not finished yet. Duncan printed that article. Not everybody has sold. They haven't found any of that os-blindium for sure. It's not over."

It sure felt like it was to Arley, who couldn't stand to watch that reptile striding around so possessively in poor little Grubstake. "I need to go," she said. "I'll see you later."

—◦◦◦◦◦◦◦—

It was too quiet at home with everybody gone and with the place already starting to feel like it wasn't quite hers anymore. Arley flapped around for a few minutes unable to start anything, and then she went looking for Anabelle. Orville and Wilbur trotted along beside her and she was glad for the company, though they might just have been hoping for more dog biscuits.

Arley rode the mule up the steep switchbacks until they reached the Never Mine. Once in a while she felt the need to come visit it, even if she couldn't go inside. Maybe because she recognized that it was a part of her history, and that she was responsible for it. Or maybe because she was getting ready to say good-bye to it.

The damage from the explosion had never been repaired, giving the place a dilapidated air, and a perilous one as well, as if the entire structure could cave in at any moment. She sat on a rock while Anabelle grazed on the few spring wildflowers that had been hardy enough to show up. The dogs chased bunnies up the slopes.

As she sat there, she heard dogs yapping and she knew it wasn't Orville and Wilbur. Around the bend came Morgan leading Millicent. Muggs and Brute were in saddlebags, yapping nonstop and happily. They must be glad to be out of that room and away from Charles Randall. Arley knew that's how she'd be feeling if she were a locked-up dog.

Morgan halted when he saw Arley. "What are you doing here?" he asked, continuing on into the clearing.

"It's my mine. What are *you* doing here?"

"This is *your* mine?"

"I thought you and Charles Randall knew everything about everybody in town. How *do* you know so much, anyway?" She hadn't forgotten that at that first meeting Charles Randall had known everybody's name and the size of each person's property.

"I've got a list but I don't care who owns what. The information came from some guy who works for Mr. Lockwood and spent a month here about a year ago. Pretended he got off the train to stretch his legs and didn't get back on in time."

"That guy who got so attached to Everdene?"

"I did hear he'd gotten infatuated with somebody

here. That's why Mr. Lockwood wouldn't let him come back."

"Sounds like something that Mr. Lockwood would do."

Morgan looked startled. "You know him?" He lifted Muggs and Brute from the saddlebags and set them on the ground. "They need some exercise," he said, tossing a few dog biscuits into the brush. All four dogs ran off after them.

"I saw him for the first time today. I don't know him but I've heard about him."

"Nothing good, I expect," Morgan muttered.

"That's how you talk about your boss? You better not let him find out."

Morgan sat down on a rock across from Arley and looked at her without speaking for so long she began to get uncomfortable. "What?" she said, remembering how sinister he'd seemed when he first arrived. Beginning to think of him as merely a rock expert may have caused her to relax too much. "Why are you looking at me like that?" Her voice shook a little.

"Just wondering if you really know who you're dealing with."

"One of the advantages of living in a place like Grubstake is that we don't hear about *anything*. Everything I know about Sidney Lockwood I've learned in the past couple of days." She looked around for Ana-belle and the dogs, who had wandered too far off to be of any help even if they'd felt like it. She sat up straighter for courage. "So far I'm mostly mad that you and your henchmen think you can just come in here and take us over, without one thought that maybe we like things the way they are."

He raised an eyebrow at her. "You like it so much that some of you could hardly wait to sell and get out."

That made her madder still. "You don't understand what desperation and disappointment can make people do."

"Don't be so sure about that." Morgan kept looking at her, his dark eyes grave—and somehow not as in-timidating.

That gave her the nerve to say, "Okay, I know you grew up in an orphanage. Well, boo hoo. A lot of these guys have had it just as hard. And they didn't grow up to have cushy jobs with the richest man in the world, or whatever Sidney Lockwood is." She was riding on a fine head of steam now, and it felt good. "They're still having it hard."

"What about you?"

"What about me?"

"Don't you want to get out of here? What about those rooms that say London and Paris and all? What about those books you read? Don't you want some of those adventures?"

"I'm having a big enough adventure right now, thank you very much." She wasn't about to let him talk her into leaving Grubstake before she knew how he'd done it.

They became aware of a lot of barking and howling going on somewhere. Arley jumped up. "Uh-oh. I'm afraid Wilbur and Orville have gotten after your dogs."

"They're in the mine," Morgan said, going to the dark mouth of the Never Mine. "All of them. Way in, from the sound of it."

"Oh, no," Arley said, alarmed. "There was an explosion a few years ago and everything's very unstable in there. Something could fall on them, or trap them. Wilbur! Orville!" she called. With their usual degree of obedience, neither dog showed up. "Call yours!"

"Muggs! Brute! Here, dogs! Come here!" But they didn't come either, which surprised Arley since they'd seemed so submissive, at least to Charles Randall's voice.

"Something in there's got them all excited," Morgan said. "We'd better go see what it is."

"No," Arley said, backing away. "It's dangerous in there. We don't have any light. The Indian spirits won't like it."

"What Indian spirits?"

"It's a legend in Grubstake. The Indians who lived here are still hanging around, making sure anybody messing in their old hunting ground is pure of heart. Or something like that."

"The Indians are still here?"

"Not the real Indians. Their spirits."

"You believe that?"

She shrugged. "I guess. I've known it all my life. They seem a little temperamental sometimes. Unpredictable. Or else their idea of pure of heart is different from mine."

The dogs kept barking like lunatics.

"Well, if that's who those dogs are barking at, shouldn't we go in and get them?"

"You go. I'll...I'll watch Millicent and Anabelle."

Morgan took a good hard look at her. "You're afraid to go in a mine," he said, getting it. "You're not afraid of Sidney Lockwood and what he can do to you with all the resources at his disposal, but you're afraid to go in a place folks with a lot less spunk and vinegar than you go every day." Then he laughed in a way that made her want to smack him good.

"If you're so anxious to have a ton of rocks fall in on you, be my guest," Arley said, embarrassed and indignant.

"All right." He rummaged in his saddlebags until he found some candles. He lit one, stuck a few extras in his boots, and entered the mine. Arley waited outside, unable to stand still as his tiny light disappeared into the darkness. She heard him calling all the dogs by their names, but they just kept barking and barking and barking, more and more faintly. Then they stopped altogether and Arley thought her heartbeat would stop, too, in pure anxiety.

Morgan was gone for a long time after the dogs quit barking, and Arley was sure she'd never see any of them again. She stood in the adit to the mine, but couldn't make herself go any farther no matter how much she gritted her teeth and tried to push her feet ahead. She wept and wrung her hands, but she couldn't go in and she couldn't leave until she found out what had happened to poor Orville and Wilbur. Oh yes, and to Morgan, Muggs, and Brute, too.

She'd given up her last shred of hope and was about to take Anabelle and Millicent back down the mountain when Morgan emerged followed by the four dogs— and all five looked quite pleased with themselves.

Arley jumped up and down in aggravation. "What happened in there? What took so long? Are the dogs all right? Why didn't you yell to me that you were alive?"

"I didn't think you cared if I was alive." Morgan,

usually so grim, really looked like a boy when he smiled. The way he was doing now.

"I don't. I meant Orville and Wilbur. And maybe Muggs and Brute. But not you. Now, are you going to tell me what was going on in there?"

The dogs took off down the mountain after a bunny whose worst nightmare, Arley imagined, must be coming true.

"You'll find out soon enough."

"You found something in there, didn't you? What you were looking for?"

"Let's just say it looks like an explosion in there revealed something surprising. And now you could ask Mr. Lockwood for any amount you want for your mine."

It took a moment for Arley to realize what he meant. Then she had to exercise all the willpower she had not to jump around screaming, "I've got pay dirt!" Instead, she said, "That must be osblindium, right?"

"What if it is? Does that mean you'll sell?"

"What if I don't?"

"Then I think you'll be seeing more of Archie than you'd like."

A cold shiver ran down Arley's back. "Well, you better hurry back to town and tell Mr. Lockwood what you found. Get Archie all fired up." She was trying so hard to keep her voice from trembling that her throat hurt.

"I do things in my own time," he said, mounting Millicent. "I'll tell Mr. Lockwood when I'm ready. That mine is still yours." And he went off down the mountain, Millicent delicately picking her way between the rocks on the path while Arley wondered what he meant about doing things in his own time. Why would he delay telling Mr. Lockwood the news he'd been waiting for? Oooh, he was so aggravating!

When she got back to town she found everybody gathered at the Spittoon, acting as if there was something to celebrate, mesmerized by Mr. Lockwood, who was at his charismatic best.

"He's making them all feel like millionaires," Everdene said with disgust. "They all imagine they can live like he does. He's not telling them that won't happen unless they're as crooked as the trail leading up to the mines."

Duncan went around with paper and pencil getting statements of reaction to Mr. Lockwood's visit from people who really had little to say but kept saying it a lot. It confirmed what Arley had noticed often before—give a person a chance to speak and they'll tell you lots more than you really want to hear.

He also followed a busy Bridget around, pressing her for an interview, though Arley couldn't really see what she'd have to add to the present situation.

Everdene would be the one with things to say about Mr. Lockwood.

Purvis, Prairie Martin, and Outdoor John were all sitting together at a table near the stairs. "Hi, Arley," said Purvis. "We're trying to decide what to do. What do you think?"

"I have no idea," she said. These guys were going to have to learn to figure things out for themselves. She wasn't going to be with them to help forever. Besides, she really *didn't* have any idea—for them or for herself.

"What?" Prairie Martin said. "But you always help us."

"If you sell your mines and leave, I won't be around to help you. Same thing if I sell the Never Mine and leave. You've got to learn to do it for yourselves."

They looked up at her with big moist eyes, the way Orville and Wilbur did (for a few seconds) when she scolded them, and she felt just terrible and mean. But she made herself move toward the bar and away from them.

"I guess you won't get to shoot Mr. Lockwood," Arley said to Everdene, "now that Archie has your gun."

"I'm still armed. He gave it back."

Arley's mouth dropped open. "He gave it back? He's not a very smart bodyguard, then, if you ask me. Or else he's as bewitched by you as every other man in the world. Except Sidney Lockwood, I guess."

"I don't know what he was thinking. He just slipped it to me behind the bar and said maybe I'd have another use for it. Did he suppose I'd want it for a paperweight? Or a doorstop? Maybe he's even dumber than we thought. So I'm still armed and dangerous."

"You're not *really* going to shoot him, are you?"

Everdene shrugged. "Maybe. I might get my chance tonight. He's having his whole gang for dinner in the railroad car. I could get him through the window while that thug of his is busy with his soup. My wrist still hurts," she said, rubbing it.

"I'll go with you."

"You will? Why? You want to shoot somebody, too?"

"No. I don't even own a gun. And I don't want you to shoot anybody either. We've already got enough trouble. I just want to snoop. I think Morgan's found osblindium in the Never Mine. But he wouldn't tell me anything for sure and he said he wasn't ready to tell Mr. Lockwood. Why not, that's my question. Isn't that why he's here—to find stuff and tell Mr. Lockwood?"

TWELVE

ONCE IT WAS DARK, and Lockwood, Charles Randall, Morgan, and Archie had departed for the railroad car, Everdene left Bridget in charge of the Spittoon. She and Arley furtively made their way down to the train station.

"You think he's got guards posted?"

"If this was somewhere besides Grubstake, I'd guess yes. But he doesn't believe we're enough of a threat to worry about, in spite of my derringer." Everdene patted her pocket. "So I bet Archie'll be inside having dinner with the guard dog and the rest of them."

Arley wasn't in favor of plugging Mr. Lockwood—

at least not fatally. But she didn't feel like arguing any more with an armed Everdene.

Parked on a siding across from the rickety little station was a shiny black locomotive attached to a shiny green private car. By the light coming from the car's windows, they could see LOCKWOOD LTD. painted in gold letters on the car's side. Though the air was damp and chilly, it wasn't actually raining, so the windows of the car were half-open—probably to dissipate the cloud of cigar smoke from inside.

"That's another reason I told him good-bye," Everdene whispered. "As if the crookedness wasn't enough, he started smoking. Cigars. Indoors. Too bad I didn't have my little pistol then. It would have saved everybody a lot of trouble."

Arley waved her hand in front of her face to clear the smoke. "This should help hide us," she said. "If we can keep from coughing."

They edged under one of the open windows and pressed themselves up against the side of the car.

The first voice they heard was Morgan's. "I don't know why you had to come all this way to fire me in person. You could have done it by telegram."

"Number one, I wanted to see for myself what you've been doing—or haven't been doing. And number two, it's more satisfying to fire somebody in person. I get to see the look on his face when I do it."

There was the sound of silverware clinking on plates.

"I know you need your salary," Mr. Lockwood continued. "And I know why you need it. So I would think you'd be more cooperative."

"I can't make the stuff be where you want it to be."

"Number one, how hard are you trying? And number two, what's the big idea letting word get out to these miners that they may be sitting on something valuable? That's going to make it more expensive for me to buy their mines."

"I can't try any harder than I'm trying. And I didn't tell anybody anything. I don't know where that information in the paper came from. But even if I had said something, I see nothing wrong with it. No one's telling them they definitely have something valuable. Not all of them will. Maybe none of them will."

"Number one, you're giving them hope, which interferes with hopelessness, which is how I want them feeling." And here Mr. Lockwood's voice got so loud that Arley tried to take a step backward even though she was already backed against the train. "And number two, you're interfering with my plans! That stuff is *here*! You said it would be! It has to be!"

Arley felt oddly as if she wanted to defend Morgan. She knew *she* wouldn't like being yelled at that way even if she had done something very bad, which she wasn't sure Morgan had. Anyway, he was apparently being fired. Wasn't that bad enough without the yelling? She just couldn't figure out why Morgan wouldn't tell Mr. Lockwood what he'd found.

"So why are you really firing me?" Morgan asked. "Because you're impatient? Because you need *more* money when you've already got so much it should be a crime—and the way you got some of it *was* a crime? Who else is going to look for it if not me? Charles Randall? He wouldn't know a nugget of osblindium if it fell in his lap."

He finally said that word out loud! Arley did a little jig on tiptoe in the dark.

Everdene mouthed, "It's really osblindium?" with her eyebrows all the way up.

Arley nodded as Charles Randall exclaimed, "I would, too!"

"Number one," Mr. Lockwood went on, "you're not the only geologist in the world. And number two, Charles Randall is useful in other ways. He's very persuasive in making sales."

"That's right," said Charles Randall emphatically. "I am."

"I'm the only geologist in Grubstake," Morgan said quietly. "This week. For an impatient person."

"Then *find* the stuff. You must be getting close by now."

"I thought I didn't work for you anymore."

Mr. Lockwood made a strangled sound. "All right, all right. You're rehired. But just until—number one— you find that stuff or—number two—I find another geologist."

"What if I don't want to work for you anymore? What if my distaste for you and your methods is just too much for me to swallow anymore?"

There was a moment of silence during which Arley practically had to yank herself by the back of her own dress to keep herself from trying to jump up and peek in the window to see Mr. Lockwood's expression. And she nearly put her hand over her own mouth to keep from cheering for Morgan.

Mr. Lockwood spoke. "My methods have made a lot of money for me. And, oh yes, have given jobs to many people. What's wrong with that?"

"What's wrong is the way you've done it," Morgan said. "Lying to people, cheating them, thinking about yourself first and only."

"Oh, that," Mr. Lockwood said casually. "That's just

business. That's how it's done. I'm not the only one doing it that way."

"How many other people are doing it isn't the point. And you must know that."

"Hey. Do you want your job back or not? Because you're doing a pretty good job of talking me out of the offer."

"I need the money and you know it. But as soon as I don't, you won't have to fire me. I'll quit."

"One, you're always going to need my money. And two, quitting is a luxury you're not ever going to have. Now, I need some more coffee. Charles! Archie! Somebody! Get me some coffee!"

Arley wished she could be the one to go pour the coffee—into Mr. Lockwood's lap. She looked over at Everdene. She was tempted to tell her to go ahead and put a bullet right into one or two of his most vital organs.

"Drat! The window's too high," Everdene whispered. "I can't get a good bead on him. I've been looking for something I can stand on so I can see better, but I can't find anything. Dang it!" She motioned to Arley. "Let's go. We've heard plenty."

They slipped away from the train and as soon as they could speak in normal voices, Everdene said, "You were right about Morgan. He really doesn't want to tell Sidney anything. I don't blame him."

"But he's stuck with his job because he needs the money even though he feels the same way you do about Mr. Lockwood."

"That's another thing. *Why* does he need the money so badly?"

"Everdene," Arley said, "we've lived without money for so long we've forgotten how important it is for just about everybody else. And once I heard him say he's supporting a lot of people."

"Who?"

"I don't know. Maybe he has a lot of children. Or impoverished relatives, like in *Peril on the Plains*. No, wait, he's an orphan."

"At least we know there's osblindium. In the Never Mine. Which means you're rich! You won't have to do without money anymore."

"Don't forget it has to be extracted, which is difficult and expensive. I can't afford to hire someone to do it. I don't know how to do it myself. And I can't even go into the Never Mine. I'll still have to sell, and I refuse to sell to Mr. Lockwood. Why isn't anything ever simple around here?" she asked, forgetting how simple things had been for so long.

Everdene put her arm around Arley's shoulders. "You need some sleep."

--◦-◦-◉-◦-◉-◦-◦--

Yet Arley couldn't sleep. She tried. But she flopped around so much Orville and Wilbur jumped off the bed and went downstairs where it wasn't so bouncy. She followed them, and the three of them were sitting by the fire when Morgan came in. The dogs scrambled to their feet, deserting Arley and swarming over Morgan as if he were their oldest friend.

"Good evening," Morgan said.

"Enjoy your dinner?" she asked, hoping she wouldn't give away anything she'd overheard.

"Not especially." Instead of going straight upstairs, he lingered, petting the dogs, who pressed against him.

"Didn't enjoy your dinner companions?" She realized that any fear she might still have had of him had completely gone away. The last shred of it had evaporated when she'd heard him tell Mr. Lockwood how he felt about him.

"Can't say that I did."

"Did you tell Mr. Lockwood whatever it was you found in my mine?" She made her eyes big and innocent.

"I'm pretty sure a snoopy girl like you knows exactly what I found."

"A snoopy...what do you mean?" She hoped she sounded more outraged than guilty, and that her eyes still looked innocent, but she wouldn't have put money on it.

"I know you've been in my room and I know where the newspaper got that statement about what could be in the mines. You think I don't take precautions?"

"What kind of precautions? Like a hair across the door frame?" That was how they did it in *The Locked Room*. She couldn't help wanting to know how a real varmint would do it.

"And across the drawers. And a thin film of powder on the floor that shows footprints. And a couple of other things I'm not going to tell you about."

"Okay, then," she said. When caught out, sometimes the best thing to do was just to admit it and not look even dumber by trying to deny something obvious. "So you wanted me to find that report? You wanted the miners to get warned?"

"It seemed fairer that way. I don't want to do business the way Lockwood Ltd. does. So what are you going to do with your valuable mine now?"

"I'm never selling it to Mr. Lockwood, that's for sure."

"Good. Don't. I'm not going to be the one responsible for letting him ruin what's left of this town."

"You aren't? I thought that was your job."

He dropped into a chair before the fire. "It is." He put his head into his hands. "Sometimes I make myself sick."

No villain in any Penny Dreadful had ever acted like that. Arley didn't know what to do. But Orville and Wilbur did. They went to Morgan and laid their muzzles on his knees.

"Then you need to quit that job," Arley said after a long silence. The habit of telling her boarders what to do was a hard one to break. "You shouldn't be doing work that's making you sick. I know Mr. Lockwood thinks he can buy anything, including your life. But he's wrong."

"You don't understand," Morgan said, his voice muffled by his hands. "I need that paycheck. That big, fat, corrupting, entrapping paycheck."

She waved her hand and shrugged. "None of my other boarders pay every bit of their room and board. I guess you could get away with that, too."

"It's not me. It's all the others."

"The others? What others?" In his distraught state, he just might tell her.

The dogs each put a paw up onto Morgan's knees. He made a gulpy sound and said, "The orphans."

Arley scratched her head. "Orphans?"

"I support the orphanage where I grew up. The benefactor they had—the one who paid for my education, and who took me with him to London—died broke. They need my paycheck."

"But nobody wants to grow up in an orphanage. Why do you want to keep it in business?"

He raised his head. His scar was white against his tanned cheek. "Abandoned on the street is a worse place for children."

She had to take his word for it. There hadn't been children in Grubstake for a long time so, except for her own admittedly odd childhood, she knew nothing about being a child, on the street or anywhere else.

She stood up. Action always made her feel better. She paced around for a while as Morgan stroked the dogs' heads absentmindedly.

"Here's what I think," she finally said. "You need another job. Not with Mr. Lockwood. We've got to fix it so he doesn't need you, and then you can go somewhere else to work. I get that he's a hard person to push around, so we need to think of a smart way to do it— one that doesn't involve Everdene shooting him full of holes."

At that, Morgan looked over at her, his dark eyes brighter and more hopeful.

"No!" Arley insisted. "As good as that sounds, it would make more trouble than we've already got, so quit looking like that would solve the problem."

"You don't want him for an enemy. He plays dirty."

"It's a little too late to worry about that, isn't it?"

Thirteen

THE NEXT MORNING ARLEY and Morgan, Wilbur and Orville crossed the muddy street on the way to the *Expositor*. The sun appeared intermittently between the clouds, and the wind blew with an edge of winter still to it. Not that the dogs seemed to notice. As long as there were puddles to splash through they were happy.

"This is the craziest spring I can remember. Seems like the weather's trying to go backward to winter. Ever since Charles Randall came to town."

"I came at the same time," Morgan said. "I could be responsible."

She looked him over. He definitely looked capable of scaring spring away with his black clothes and his scar.

Duncan was laboring over another of his happy-ending mining stories when Arley and Morgan came into the office.

"We need to talk to you about something," Arley said without preamble.

Duncan jumped to his feet when he saw her with Morgan. He grabbed a letter opener on his desk and opened his mouth but nothing came out.

"Morgan says there's osblindium in the mines here for sure. That's what Mr. Lockwood has been looking for. He needs it for his paint and textile business. He's been trying to get at it cheaply before the miners know it's there. In other words, he's been cheating them. We mostly knew all that, but now Morgan is on our side. And he's going to help us do something about it."

Maybe it was the tonic effect of having a guy who looked like an outlaw at her side, but she had no trouble talking to Duncan at all.

"I don't know what I can be expected to do," Duncan said, setting down the letter opener. "I published a special broadsheet that went entirely ignored. Perhaps you are underestimating how much the remaining residents of Grubstake want out."

"But this time you can say there's osblindium in there for sure. Morgan found it. There might be a lot of it."

"Probably," Morgan said.

"And you think my publishing this confirmation will do *what*? Make the miners feel more possessive about their mines? They still will have neither the resources nor the expertise to actually mine the osblindium. I believe publishing confirmation will only enable them to ask for more money from Mr. Lockwood. And if he is desirous enough of possessing these mines, he'll pay it. Then you, and undoubtedly a few other holdouts, will have the privilege of living on property surrounded by land owned by the last person on earth you would want for a neighbor."

"Huh," Arley said, thinking. "But!" She raised a finger. "We know what'll happen if we do nothing. Lockwood will wear them down for sure. It's worth one more try, I say. We can tell them to sell, if they have to, to anybody but him. Think, Duncan. This is what it's like to be a real newspaperman! Printing something important, something that could change minds and lives. Something that feels dangerous."

"Of course. You're right. Crusading journalists are never discouraged by long odds or strong opposition. Let's get to it." He sat back down at his desk.

They were all still there when Lacey came marching into the *Expositor* office, casting a glance at Arley and Morgan, and then ignoring them.

"Hello, Duncan. I have a big decision to make, so I'm having a tea party. You have to come."

"I do? When is it?"

"I have to decide soon, so—now."

Duncan jumped away from the press where he had just begun printing the special edition. "Now? That's impossible. This might be the most significant story the *Expositor* has ever run," he said, casting a look at Arley for confirmation. "It's vital that I get it out. I'll have to drink tea some other time."

"Not with me." Lacey's blue eyes were hard as marbles. "I've found somebody else who takes tea seriously. Thank you for helping me make my final choice." And she whisked out the door, her pink dimity flouncing.

"Choice?" he said to the closed door.

"Looks like you were in the running for something you didn't know about," Morgan said. "I'd say *you're* the one who won."

Duncan looked at him for a moment until the press clanked. Then he turned back to his work.

—◦◦◦◦◦—

Later Morgan sat at the kitchen table doing nothing while Arley, in a frenzy of agitation, scrubbed the cast-iron cook stove smooth and reblacked it. "I feel like I'm waiting for a dynamite explosion," she said.

"That's what it'll be like," Morgan said. He cleared his throat. "Look. I know you've got this bulldog idea that if you just keep trying you can outwit Lockwood, but I think you read too many of those books of yours. He's demolished bigger competition than you."

"So I shouldn't even try?" She paused, a dirty rag in her hand. "Do you hear something? It sounds like... like somebody bellowing."

Morgan listened. "Lockwood probably."

Orville and Wilbur came out from under the kitchen table where they'd been staying out of Arley's agitated way, pricked up their ears, and began to howl along with the bellowing. They were still at it when Mr. Lockwood burst through the kitchen door waving the single sheet of newsprint that was Duncan's second special edition.

"You're the 'unimpeachable source' who's found os-blindium and you didn't tell me?" he bellowed. The dogs changed their tune from howling to snarling, but they kept their distance from the shouting man.

Morgan nodded calmly.

"You're fired!" Lockwood shouted.

"I quit."

Mr. Lockwood grabbed the front of Morgan's shirt and hauled him to his feet. "You...you..."

That's the problem with knowing a lot of bad words,

Arley thought. *Too many choices.* Sometimes it was hard to decide which one to use.

The dogs growled louder.

"Take your hands off me," Morgan said, wrestling his shirt out of Mr. Lockwood's grip. "I'm not your employee anymore."

"Or what?" Mr. Lockwood sneered. "This burg doesn't even have a sheriff to complain to."

"That's because Grubstake didn't have any crime to speak of. Until you showed up," Arley said, wondering if it was time to start fumbling for her knife again.

"I've committed no crimes," Mr. Lockwood said self-righteously.

"What about assault?" said Arley. "What about swindling...swindlement...whatever it's called... when you cheat someone out of something you know about but they don't."

"I had no concrete knowledge of anything when I had Charles Randall make those offers."

Oh, the guy is slippery, Arley thought. "Well, I'm sure you did something wrong even if I'm not one hundred percent sure what it is," she said.

"I'd like to see you prove that. I'd have my lawyers on you so fast you wouldn't know what hit you."

Oooh, he was making her so mad! She gave a hand signal to the snarling dogs, and for once they obeyed her instruction, leaping directly onto Mr. Lockwood. He fell under a pile of fur. While he struggled and bellowed, the dogs sat on him, looking eagerly to Arley for approval.

"Good boys," she told them.

Morgan smoothed the front of his black shirt and said to her, "This will accomplish nothing, no matter how satisfying it is."

Arley sighed. "Oh, all right. Let him up, boys."

Reluctantly the dogs got off Mr. Lockwood and Morgan jerked him to his feet.

"You'll pay for this," Mr. Lockwood threatened. "Both of you. And those mutts, too. I'll make mincemeat out of them." He brushed himself off and headed for the door. "Oh. And just so you know—I bought two more mines since I've been here. You're not convincing anybody not to sell. Sooner or later I'll buy one that has what I want in it."

"I know one you'll never get," Arley shot back. "And it's the most valuable one of all."

Both Morgan and Mr. Lockwood looked startled.

"So," Mr. Lockwood said. "The Never Mine is where you found the osblindium. Well, well, well." He tipped his hat and went out the door.

Arley put her hand over her mouth.

"Too bad you didn't do that about fifteen seconds

ago," Morgan said. "Now you're in for it. He knows which mine he really has to have."

"Well, he'll never get it. I'd die before I'd sell it to him."

Morgan just kept looking at her until she heard what she'd just said. "No! You don't mean he'd kill me to get my mine. Do you?"

"I wouldn't put it past him," Morgan said. "He wants what he wants and he doesn't care how he gets it."

"But not...I mean, he wouldn't stoop to...would he?"

Morgan shrugged. "If he doesn't want to do his own dirty work, he's got Archie."

Penny Dreadfuls had always a happy ending, which was one reason Arley loved them. But real life, she was starting to see, wasn't so cooperative.

Feeling like Prairie Martin, she said, "What should I do?"

"The way I see it," Morgan said, "you have three choices. You can sell your mine. Or you can sit tight and wait for him to get it away from you some other way. Or you can try to think of some scheme to make him change his mind and go away." He gave a skeptical laugh.

"Well, I'm not selling, so it'll have to be one of those other choices. After all, he's not superhuman. He's just a regular man. He puts his pants on one leg at a time."

But her mind formed a picture of Mr. Lockwood vaulting into his pants both legs at once.

"Then I suggest you be very, very careful. He knows what you've got and he wants it and he's capable of anything."

Her little knife and her seldom-obedient dogs were seeming like pretty puny protection just then. And her miners! They weren't home yet, but she had them to look out for, too. Purvis would have so much trouble understanding what was going on, and Prairie Martin would never be able to decide what to do, and Outdoor John would be so frightened he'd be useless.

Her shoulders sagged with the responsibility.

"I can help," Morgan said. "After all, I'm unemployed."

And then she remembered the orphans. Who would take care of them now? But she wasn't going to mention them. He already knew he'd put them at risk.

⚬⦿·⊙⚬

Late that afternoon when Arley was starting supper, she heard a dog whining at the back door. It wouldn't be either Wilbur or Orville. They just barged in, and if the door was closed they threw themselves against it until someone heard and came to open it.

Arley put down her spoon and went to see what was going on. When she opened the door, there lay Orville and Wilbur on the doorstep, sodden with rainwater, tied together by a rope around their necks, gasping and whining and foaming at the mouth. She knew right away what had happened, and she directed a few choice bad words at herself for not having seen it coming.

She grabbed them by their scruffs, heaved them in out of the rain, cut the rope with the pocketknife she was, for once, able to get out of her pocket, took the pot off the fire, grabbed her shawl, and, leaving the dogs in a miserable huddle on the kitchen floor, ran for Wing's.

Bursting in the door, she cried, "I think my dogs have been poisoned. You've got to come quick."

Without a word, Wing threw some things into a satchel and followed her out into the rain and back to the house. The dogs looked even worse than they had when she left. They lay panting and wheezing and foaming. While Arley was fetching Wing, Outdoor John had returned home and was there in the kitchen wringing his hands in distress but also, Arley thought, looking at the dogs with a bit too much of a taxidermist's interest.

"What happened?" he asked. "What's wrong with them?"

"They've been poisoned," Arley said, pushing him out of the way.

"Are you sure? Maybe they just ate something rotten. They've done that before."

Indeed they had. Many times. Their digestive systems, in fact, were usually objects of admiration. But they'd never looked this bad, no matter what they'd eaten.

Wing sent her to do things with towels and hot water and basins while he began mixing ingredients. Getting the mixture into the dogs was quite a struggle considering how weak they were. But, oh my, getting the mixture out was easy, though explosive, and odorific, and voluminous, and sent Outdoor John scampering out of the kitchen. However, as soon as the double-ended explosions were over, the dogs tottered to their feet and wanted to lean against Arley for support. They were such a mess she didn't want to touch them, but how could she deny them any comfort after what they'd been through? She shrugged and let them lean. She'd just leave her clothes in the woodshed until wash day. But she did put on her heaviest work gloves—the ones she used to handle the miners' laundry—to pet them. Wing washed them gently with warm water as they leaned, wobbly, against her knees.

"Do you know what was wrong with them?" she asked. "Will they be okay?"

"Poison, no question. I know the smell. Emptying is best treatment."

"I don't see how they could be any emptier," Arley said. "This kitchen's going to take forever to clean up. Supper's going to be late tonight."

"I help," Wing said. "Besides, need to stay to see how they doing."

By the time the kitchen was cleaned up, all the miners and Morgan had returned. Over supper, Arley had to tell them what she and Wing believed had happened to the dogs, and why, and who was responsible.

Outdoor John put his fork down and pushed his chair away from the table. "What are we going to do?" he cried in a high voice. "He's a very bad man."

"Yes, that's true," Arley said, trying to sound calm even though she wanted to squeal and run away, too. "So we'll just have to be very careful and stay alert and carry weapons. He's just a man," she reminded them. "He puts his pants on one leg at a time."

"I bet he can do it two legs at a time," Prairie Martin said glumly. "Shouldn't we just sell him our mines and get it over with? He's going to kill us all and take them away from us anyway."

"Now, we're not going to think like that," said Arley,

who'd been thinking exactly like that. "We're going to keep fighting him, right?"

There was dead silence around the table.

"Right?" she said louder.

"Do you smell fire?" Purvis asked, sniffing loudly. "Not from the fireplace, I mean?"

The dogs, too, had lifted their noses and taken a few sniffs.

Morgan was on his feet before anyone, and out the back door. The others followed, their napkins still tucked into their shirt collars. They dashed out just in time to see him throwing a bucket of rainwater onto the side of the shed where the firewood was kept. A merry little blaze under the eave was extinguished before it had done more than scorch the side of the shed, but all of them were imagining what could have happened if the fire had taken hold. The nice dry firewood inside would have started a conflagration big enough to take the house down with it.

"Mr. Lockwood," Prairie Martin said. "And Archie." All the others nodded.

"He just meant to scare us this time," Morgan said.

"Well, it worked," Outdoor John said in a little voice.

"He knew we'd all be here having supper," Morgan went on, "so we'd discover it in time. It was just a warning."

"I'm warned," Purvis said. "For once, I don't need any explanations."

"Remember that saying you wrote down?" Arley asked him. "Remember, 'Plan ahead or find trouble on the doorstep'?"

"Oh. Yes. Wing told me that. Well, here it is. On our doorstep."

"But what about the 'plan ahead' part? We have to think about that now."

"But how are we supposed to know what he'll do next? We're up at our mines all alone, in the dark, every day."

"Don't go to mines," Wing said. "Why borrow trouble? It comes by itself."

"Well said," Morgan commented. "It's come and it's brought friends."

"Why don't we go back in and finish our supper instead of standing out here in the dark and the damp?" Arley said.

Dutifully they trooped back inside, but nobody had any appetite. Orville and Wilbur happily filled themselves up again on the leftovers.

Everyone trudged drearily off to bed where they jumped every time the house creaked in the wind. No one slept a wink.

ᚠOURTEEN

FOLLOWING WING'S ADVICE, nobody went to the mines the next morning. Arley couldn't blame them. Mines were scary enough without the thought of Archie lurking inside, waiting.

Orville and Wilbur stuck close to Arley all morning. Every time she sat down to try to lose her worries in *Rustler's Rhapsody* they wanted to get in her lap. When she went upstairs they were crowded so close to her that she was afraid they'd all end up in a heap at the bottom of the steps. She hated seeing her juvenile delinquent dogs so feeble and clingy. It wasn't good for their morale. Or for her balance.

By afternoon she was stir-crazy. The boarders had

gotten tired of card games and tiddlywinks, and had gone up to their rooms to nap. Morgan had been in his room since breakfast. She decided to go see Everdene and Bridget and tell them what was going on instead of just waiting for something to happen.

When she left the house the dogs hung back at the door, wanting to come along, but afraid to step outside their sanctuary. That made her as mad at Sidney Lockwood as everything else had. She had no choice but to leave them behind.

As Arley hurried along the wood sidewalk, clutching her shawl and looking all around, she peeked in the window of the *Expositor* and saw Duncan on his hands and knees. What was he doing? Praying? Playing horsie? She pushed the door open and went in.

"Duncan? What are you doing?"

When he sat back on his haunches, she could see that the floor was covered with little metal cubes of type—the letters of all different sizes that Duncan set up in frames to print the paper. The fact that he had to do it backwards to get it to print frontwards always amazed her.

"Somebody broke in here last night and dumped all my type out on the floor. There must be nine hundred pieces that have to be sorted and put back in their proper places. It'll take me forever."

"I can help." Arley squatted and picked up one little piece, turning it around trying to read it. Backwards was bad enough—it was so small she couldn't tell if it was even right side up. "Oh."

"That's all right. Nobody can decipher these things as well as I can. I've had years of experience. But who would commit such an act? Why?"

"Come on, Duncan. Think who might be upset that you printed things in the newspaper about what he's trying to do to Grubstake? Who's new in town who might be responsible for something that never happened before when it was just us Grubs?"

"Oh. Of course. But that's so . . . so malicious. And vitriolic. And insidious."

"And that's not all," Arley said. "Last night somebody set fire to my shed, and tried to poison Orville and Wilbur, too."

"Are you convinced they didn't just eat something putrid? They've done that before."

She stood. "Yes, I'm sure. Wing recognized the poison. Somebody's trying very hard to get us to quit making trouble."

Duncan knelt at her feet, his hands full of type. "Well, he can't shut down the power of the press." His voice was full of strength, and passion, and some of whatever it was that could make her feel all tongue-tied and twittery. Only this time nothing twittery happened. And her tongue stayed untied.

"Huh," she mused. What was that all about? She still admired Duncan's dedication, and his brains, and his splendid looks, but something was missing—the something that had made her act like such a ninny in front of him.

"What?" He looked up from the scattered type.

"Nothing," Arley said. And that's really what it was. Nothing. Had she been making Duncan a character in her own personal Penny Dreadful? And now that she was experiencing the real thing, with real villains and heroes and outlaws, she didn't need to pretend about him anymore? Had she just gotten tired of trying to understand him? Or now that Lacey didn't want him, did he seem less desirable? Who knew? All she could tell was that the fizz was gone—and she didn't miss it. When you were worried about getting knocked off by a ruthless tycoon or one of his henchmen, it was kind of hard to think about romance.

"See you later, Duncan. Good luck with the type." And she crossed the street to the Spittoon.

—◦·◉·◉·◦—

Bridget was standing at the bar folding towels, but Everdene was nowhere in sight.

"Hey, Bridget," Arley said. "You got time for a sarsaparilla?"

"Sure." She poured them each a glass. "Come sit down at a table."

"Where is everybody?"

"Everdene and Archie are in the storeroom. He's cleaning it out and moving things around in there for her."

"Archie?" Arley jumped to her feet. "Are you nuts? He's dangerous. Everdene shouldn't be alone with him!"

"Calm down," Bridget said. "Archie's as besotted as all the other miners. If she wanted him to stand on his head, he'd do it. Anyway, I'm keeping an eye out. The door's open and every time I go by there I look in. She's sitting on a box, calm as you please, while Archie sweats and makes sheep's eyes at her."

Arley sat down again. "If you say so." Then she told Bridget about the dogs and the fire and Duncan's type. "Sounds like Archie's work to me."

"This is bad. Mr. Lockwood's getting serious and playing dirty. We all need to be alert and careful. But I still don't think Archie would hurt Everdene."

Duncan came through the front doors in his shirt-sleeves, his tie askew. "I'm sick of straightening out type." He fell into a chair at the table. "Can I have one of whatever you're drinking?"

Bridget brought him a glass of sarsaparilla. "Are you afraid?" she asked him.

He looked straight into her eyes and said, "That's the most extraordinary question anyone has ever asked me."

For a moment Arley wished she'd thought to ask him that. And then she was glad she hadn't.

"Are you?" Bridget asked again, looking right back at him.

"Almost every day. Even more lately. Are you?"

"Almost every day. Even more lately. As Wing says, life is precarious, even at its best."

"He's right. What are you most afraid of?"

"Freezing. Starving. Being alone. Rabbits."

"Rabbits. Me, too!"

They looked into each other's eyes some more as Arley realized Duncan was speaking like a regular person, without his big words. And Bridget! Competent, sensible, no-nonsense Bridget was afraid of rabbits while Arley was living with a bunch of stuffed ones without even thinking about them. How strange to think that these were people she thought she knew. Did emergencies reveal new parts of people—or just parts that had always been there that nobody took the time to pay attention to?

"What makes you feel less afraid?" Bridget asked.

"Big words. Sarsaparilla," Duncan said. And then, after a long pause, "You."

Oh! Arley thought. While she and Lacey had been having thoughts about Duncan, he hadn't been thinking about them at all.

Arley took her glass and tiptoed away, but Duncan and Bridget didn't seem to notice. Stealthily, she approached the storeroom door. If she was going to catch Archie doing anything bad, she would have to be very quiet. She flattened herself against the wall outside the storeroom and listened.

"If you'll just stack those two barrels there," she heard Everdene saying, "you can rest for a minute."

"You're as tough as Mr. Lockwood," Archie said. "But a lot prettier."

"I'm tougher," Everdene said, "by far. I have strength of character, and he doesn't even know what that is."

"I'd like to have some of that, too, then," Archie said, panting. "But I don't know what it is either. How do you get it?"

"It's simple. By doing things you can be proud of, even when they're hard and you don't want to do them. Are you proud of the work you do for Mr. Lockwood?"

"I'm real good at it. And sometimes it's hard. But a lot of times, especially lately, I don't want to do it. Can I sit down now?"

"Certainly. Here." Arley heard the clink of glass and the glug-glug of liquid being poured. "I don't doubt you're good at it," Everdene went on, "but are you proud?"

"Not everybody can do what I do." Archie sounded proud.

Everdene sighed gustily. "For heaven's sake, Archie, you're missing the point! Is what you *do* good? Not *how* you do it."

"Oh. Well, no, of course not. That's not why Mr. Lockwood hired me."

"Then you can't have a strong character. That's all there is to it."

"Are you sure?" He sounded disappointed.

"No doubt whatsoever." There was a pause and then she said, "What about not wanting to do what Mr. Lockwood tells you to do lately? That could be a start. What does he want you to do?"

"Oh, you know. The usual. Hurt people. Destroy property. Be cruel to animals."

"Jumping junebugs!" Everdene exclaimed. "You've got to stop all that. Right now, while you still have, maybe, a shred of character left!"

"But that's my job."

"There are lots of other jobs. Ones that don't require all that...what you've been doing."

"Mr. Lockwood pays real well." Archie sounded distressed.

"He better, considering he's buying your honor, your good name, your dignity, and your self-respect."

"He is?"

Everdene's voice softened. "Don't you feel it? Don't you get mad at yourself sometimes for doing what he says?"

There was a pause. "How did you know?" Archie asked quietly.

"That's what always happens when your character is being destroyed. So, see? You're not the big dumb ape you at first appear to be."

"Huh," he said thoughtfully. "I've always thought I came across as a big smart ape. But I can't quit. He... he has things on me. On all of us."

"What, you mean he knows a secret about you? He threatens you with that?"

"Well, all the things I've done for him—"

"You can make amends for that. Some of it anyway. You can make apologies. Or pay money. Is that the worst?"

"No." There was a long silence while Arley used all her willpower to keep from peeking. Everdene was silent, too. Finally Archie spoke again. "I...I killed somebody once."

"Just one person?"

"Yes!" Archie said indignantly. "What do you take me for?"

Everdene stayed quiet.

"Anyway, it was an accident," he said. "When Mr. Lockwood was interviewing me for the job—it was in his office in Denver one night—this man ran in to attack Mr. Lockwood and I tried to protect him, just automatically—by instinct, you know—and I ended up pushing him out the window. Mr. Lockwood said he'd take care of the evidence, and nobody would ever know except him. And now he threatens to tell the police whenever I try to quit."

"Did you actually see the...the evidence?" Everdene asked.

"No. But Mr. Lockwood looked out the window—it was three floors up—and told me the fellow was a goner. Now, remember, he had a knife, so it was really self-defense."

"I've known Sidney Lockwood for a long time," Everdene said, "and I wouldn't put it past him to hire an acrobat, or an actor, or somebody like that, to burst in with a weapon, fall out the window onto a cushion or something, and then brush himself off and walk away. Just so he'd have something to threaten you with. What do you think about that?"

Archie said slowly, "I've seen him do stuff like that before. I just didn't think he'd do it to me. Was I stupid?"

"As Wing says, nobody has to stay stupid if they don't want to. Do you want to?"

"No! I guess I'm not as smart as I thought. Like Charles Randall. Everybody thinks he's so smart and so sharp and all, but he let Mr. Lockwood get something on him, too."

"Really?" Everdene said in a silky voice. "Whatever could Mr. Randall have done?"

"Oh, he's done *time*. I found out by accident once when I was waiting for Mr. Lockwood in his office and the wind blew—through that same open window!—some papers off his desk. When I picked them up I saw a report about how Randall had spent two years in the clink for selling some kind of snake oil medicine that made a lot of people sick and didn't cure anybody. He always says he can get anybody to buy anything from him, or sell anything to him—but he sure wouldn't want his customers to know he'd been in the jug for conning people."

"Well, well, well," Everdene said. "Archie, I think you're through moving boxes and barrels for today. You've got a bigger project to tackle—if you want to."

"Quitting Mr. Lockwood's employ, you mean?"

"Exactly. Do you want to?"

"More than anything. I felt terrible about poisoning those dogs."

"What dogs?" Everdene asked.

At that, Arley could no longer contain herself. She made an involuntary strangled noise that caused the storage room to go suddenly dead silent. Before Everdene or Archie could come out and find her, Arley stepped into the doorway. "Hey," she said. "What're you doing?"

Everdene gave her a narrow-eyed look. "What are *you* doing?"

Arley cleared her throat. "Uh, I was just having a sarsaparilla with Bridget and Duncan, and Bridget said you were in here, so I thought I'd come by and say hello. Hello."

"How are Orville and Wilbur?" Everdene asked.

With that question, Arley knew that Everdene understood just which dogs Archie had poisoned. And that she meant to make Archie atone for it. "Better. But they were pretty sick last night. Wing thinks they were poisoned. So do I. Who do you think could do such a thing?"

Archie looked at his shoelaces while both Arley and Everdene gave him hard glares.

"Anything else?" Everdene asked.

"A fire in the woodshed. And somebody spilled all of Duncan's type."

Everdene continued to glare at Archie, who continued to examine his shoelaces.

"Archie, you're out of a job, from this minute on, right?" Everdene asked.

"Right," Archie said meekly.

"And you're going to help us play the same kind of trick on Sidney Lockwood that he's been playing on other people," Arley said.

"How do you know—," Archie began.

"Here's your first lesson in not being stupid," Everdene said. "Knowing when to shut up. Now would be that time."

"Okay," Archie said, and shut up.

Everdene gave him a pleased look.

"We need to have a meeting with my boarders, and Duncan, and Morgan, and you, and Bridget, and Archie, and Wing, and talk about what to do," Arley said. "We can't let our poor little town—what's left of it—get taken over by that...that..."

"We know who you mean," Everdene said. "But how can we meet without him knowing about it? Bridget and I can't just close up the Spittoon."

"Why not?" Arley asked. "Have you ever taken a day off?"

"Well, there was that time a few years back when I was down with the quinsy for two days, before Bridget came. And did I ever hear about that! I *had* to get back on my feet or there'd have been a riot."

"What about putting one of the miners in charge? Or leaving a keg of beer out so they can help themselves?"

Everdene just looked at her.

"Okay, then, we'll just give them warning so they can stock up tomorrow before you close down. Just say it's a preview of how things will be in Grubstake if the town dies. There won't be anyplace to meet your pals for a drink. There won't be any *pals*. And there won't be any Everdene."

"That could work. I'll make up a sign tonight, and I'll tell them, too, since I'm not sure how many of them can read. Especially after a couple of nips."

"Why don't you just have your meeting in the morning?" Archie asked. "Mr. Lockwood wants Randall up and out early. And I'll bet there aren't any miners in here until afternoon."

Everdene and Arley looked at each other. And then Everdene said, "The second lesson in not being stupid is piping up when you've got a better idea than anybody else." She turned to Arley. "Bridget and Archie and I will be at your place in the morning. How's ten?"

—◦—◉·◎—◦—

Overnight somebody threw a rock through the window of the mercantile and removed the wheels from one of the miner's wagons. At the meeting at Arley's, Archie swore it wasn't him. He'd told Mr. Lockwood the night before he was quitting and he didn't care who he told about the guy who'd fallen out the window. Who'd believe a story like that anyway without any evidence? He sure wished he'd thought of that a lot sooner, but obviously he used to be just a big dumb ape, and he wasn't anymore. As for the other things Archie had done for Mr. Lockwood, he was going to try to make as many amends as he could.

At that, he turned to Arley and said, "I'm sorry about that fire at the woodshed. I'm glad it didn't get any bigger. And I'm really sorry about the dogs. But I have to tell you, as soon as they smelled that poisoned meat on me, they jumped me and knocked me down and took it away from me. I couldn't have stopped them if I'd tried. And Duncan, about the type—"

Duncan waved a hand dismissively. "It actually helped me get better organized. I didn't have anything

else to do anyway. And Bridget came over to help me."
He cast a fond glance in her direction and, to Arley's
amazement, Bridget, normally so cool-headed, blushed
and looked down at her hands.

"How did Mr. Lockwood take your news, Archie?"
Arley asked, passing around a plate of the cinnamon
rolls Wing had brought.

"He got purple in the face, and yelled, and threatened, and swore. About what I expected. But it felt good
to know I didn't have to do what he said anymore."

"Lesson three in not being stupid," Everdene said.
"Don't do what somebody else tells you if you know it's
not right. I'm proud of you, Archie."

Then *Archie* blushed, all the way over his bald
head. "Now I just have to worry about him coming
after me the way he does after you all."

Morgan silently nodded.

FIFTEEN

FOR THE NEXT TWO hours this select group of Grubs brainstormed and argued and restrained themselves from throwing cinnamon rolls at each other while Wing interjected sayings about peace, tranquility, and harmony, and Everdene said things about who was being stupid and how. Finally, they agreed on a plan that was mostly Arley's idea.

"Are we sure this is a good plan?" Arley asked. "Or are we just sick of arguing and want to stop speaking to each other?"

"Both, I think," Morgan said. "Now, is everybody clear on what they have to do—especially you, Purvis?"

Purvis nodded. "It's going to take me a couple of days to get ready, though."

"Then that's how long it'll take," Morgan said.

Arley couldn't help being impressed with Morgan's leadership skills. Without him guiding them, she wasn't sure if they'd all have survived the meeting, even if he did look as somber and as ominous in his black clothing as a gathering storm.

—◦◦⟨◉⟩·⟨◉⟩◦◦—

For the next day and a half, while Mr. Lockwood and Charles Randall went from mine to mine with bundles of cash, trying to buy up more property, Arley's house was strangely silent. All the miners were in their rooms working on their preparations as Morgan went from room to room checking on their progress. The dogs and Arley, whose contribution wasn't yet required, spent a lot of time huddled on her bed with a few Penny Dreadfuls scattered within reach. The whole scheme, which had seemed to make sense when they were planning it, now seemed ridiculously flimsy and dangerous and impossible.

—◦◦⟨◉⟩·⟨◉⟩◦◦—

The morning of the big day, when Arley came down to the kitchen, a note from Purvis was propped by two of

Prairie Martin's candle wax gnomes on the kitchen work table. It read: We're all behin you, Arlee. And then, in smaller print: Onlee farther bak. The border was decorated with colored inks and gold leaf with little pictures of Orville and Wilbur cavorting through puddles and petunias and laundry on the line. She didn't know how he'd had time to make it in addition to all the other things he was responsible for, unless he wasn't sleeping any more than she was.

Knowing that the whole plan depended on her to get it started tied her stomach (also liver, spleen, and gizzards) into so many knots she couldn't eat a bit of breakfast. And nobody could talk. Even the dogs seemed to feel the tension and paced uneasily around the table, their toenails clicking on the floor like buckshot.

Morgan and the boarders left after breakfast. Arley cleaned up the kitchen and then paced with the dogs until she thought the time was right.

The window of the mercantile had been patched with boards, but new glass would have to wait until the train came to pick up the order letter, and then a month after that to deliver the pane. By then there might not even be a town needing a mercantile. Arley sighed and went in.

Lacey and Mrs. Bernaise were fingering bolts of cloth disdainfully. "Inferior," Mrs. Bernaise sniffed.

Arley thought she'd just been insulted until she realized Mrs. Bernaise was referring to the cloth. "Good morning," she made herself say.

The ladies nodded to her and moved off to poke into a basket of buttons. Arley stood looking into a barrel of pickles as if they were exotic sea creatures. Just when she was contemplating bailing out on the whole project, Everdene came through the door, a basket on her arm.

"Good morning, Lacey. Belinda," she said to the Bernaises. Then, as if just noticing Arley, she said, "Oh. Good morning to you, too, Arley."

"Hey, Everdene," Arley said in a small voice, and then turned her attention back to the pickles.

Everdene strolled through the store examining items while Clarence, the proprietor, sat on a stool behind the counter keeping a close eye on Mickey, who was browsing with a fifteen-gallon hat pulled down over his ears and a glum look on his face.

As Everdene passed Arley behind a pile of donkey blankets, Arley whispered, "What's with that enormous hat on Mickey?"

Everdene bit her lip to keep from laughing. "He was sleeping on the floor at the Spittoon—you know how he does—last night when I went off to bed, and this morning we discovered that somebody had given him a very uneven haircut, bald in some spots and tufty in others. They'd even tried to cut off his eyebrows. I've got to say, as far as scare tactics, that one's pretty silly."

"I don't think Mickey sees it that way," Arley said. Then, taking a deep breath, she began the plan.

Speaking in a low voice just barely loud enough for Lacey and her mother to hear, she said, "Well, Morgan finally did it. He found what Mr. Lockwood wants."

Everdene said, "I thought Morgan got fired."

"Actually, he quit. But he was still curious, so he kept looking."

"Does Lockwood know? If he doesn't, I certainly won't tell him. You know how I feel about that man."

"I'm afraid he does know. And he even knows where it is. You'll never guess. It's in the Never Mine."

"You're kidding."

"Nope. I've got what everybody wants. I just can't afford to get it out."

By this time, Lacey and her mother were standing still as stones, listening so hard they were almost leaning toward Arley and Everdene, their fingers frozen stiff in the button basket.

"But now you can ask a lot more for your mine," Everdene said.

"I don't know, Everdene. I swore I'd never sell to

him. You know those stories the old-timers tell about the Indian spirits up in these mountains, how they let only the deserving have their bounty, and how they wreak havoc on the undeserving. Sidney Lockwood is definitely among the undeserving."

"I know what he'd say about that. He hasn't got a superstitious bone in his body."

"Even though some miners have heard sounds in their mines, found little signs and symbols meant to scare them off, and suspected that they haven't hit the mother lode because of those spirits?" Arley darted a quick glance toward Lacey and Mrs. Bernaise.

"He'd just say they were pantywaists."

"That's why I'm going to send telegrams to Lockwood's competitors, offering to sell my osblindium to them. And I'm going to send them samples so they know I've got the real stuff. I'm going up to get the samples right now. All it took was a little osblindium to get me over my fear of mines."

"That's great. Well, I better get going. Good luck." Everdene took the few things she'd picked up to the counter to pay Clarence. Before she was finished, Lacey and Mrs. Bernaise were out the door and hurrying off along the sidewalk.

Everdene turned to Arley and winked. "This might be more fun than plugging him," she said.

"We've got a long way to go," Arley said, waving her hands. "It's not fun yet."

"Huh?" Clarence said.

"Nothing," Arley said. "Nice hat," she said to Mickey. He pulled his hat down a little tighter over his eyebrows and headed out the door.

After Everdene had paid for her goods, she and Arley left the mercantile together. Down the block they could see Mrs. Bernaise, Lacey, and Charles Randall on the wooden sidewalk in front of the Spittoon. Their heads were together and Lacey was talking fast. Mrs. Bernaise looked up and saw Everdene and Arley headed their way. Quickly she grabbed Lacey's and Randall's arms and they headed away.

Arley and Everdene went into the Spittoon, where Bridget was peeking out the dusty window. "So far, I think, so good," she said, dropping the faded curtain back across the window.

"It's barely the beginning," Arley said, clenching her jaw to keep her teeth from chattering. "Now I need to pick up the dogs."

"Remember, their door is locked," Bridget said.

"Don't worry. I brought your hairpin. I can get them out."

Although Muggs and Brute growled and snapped as Arley fiddled with the lock, once she opened the door, they wagged their tails and jumped up, putting their paws on her knees. She knew she smelled of Orville and Wilbur, but that usually had the effect of keeping people at a distance, not of causing this kind of welcome. She patted their heads and scratched their ears and said, "Come on now. We've got work to do. We're going to show your master why he should never have been mean to you two."

The dogs skattled along behind her down the stairs to the door. Arley peeked out, up and down the street. Other than a few mules standing in the road, no one was in sight. "Let's go," she said. Just before she shut the door behind her, she turned back to Everdene and Bridget. "See you in a little while."

When she entered her house with Muggs and Brute, Orville and Wilbur raced up to greet them as if they were long-lost relatives. Chasing rabbits and eating dog biscuits together were apparently great bonding activities. Arley let all the dogs mill around, sniffing and licking each other for a few minutes, and then she said, "Enough with the howdy-dos. We've got work to get to." She doled out a few of Morgan's dog biscuits, put the rest in her skirt pockets, and went out the back door to get Anabelle, with the pack of dogs trailing behind her.

As Arley and Anabelle started away from the

house with Muggs and Brute in the saddlebags, Orville and Wilbur stopped at the edge of the yard. "Come on, you guys," Arley urged. "We've got to *go*."

Still they hung back—and she got mad at Mr. Lockwood all over again for putting fear of poisoning into her normally boisterous boys.

"Oh, Aunt Nellie's nightgown," she said, getting down off Anabelle. She moved Muggs into the same saddlebag as Brute, which made it pretty crowded, then heaved a trembling Wilbur into the empty one. He went in only about halfway, but she was hoping it was enough so that he wouldn't fall out. Then she laid Orville across Anabelle and mounted up behind him. Anabelle looked back in disgust at what appeared to be a carnival act before she began trudging up the track to the Never Mine, pretending she knew nothing about all the dogs on her back.

The area around the mine appeared so deserted when Arley arrived that she wondered if she'd gotten her instructions wrong. Still, she unloaded all the dogs, who stayed so close that she kept tripping over them as she led Anabelle off the trail to hide her behind a big tumble of rocks. There she found Millicent tied up along with a bunch of mules, including Purvis's Burrito and Outdoor John's Mrs. Jones. She stumbled over dogs on her way back to the mine, where all still seemed derelict and abandoned—just the way it was supposed to.

She went to the mine entrance and called softly, "Helloooo in there. Anybody home?"

After a long silence, while the air inside the mine seemed to be breathing, a faint sound began, a sort of high wailing that became louder and eerier before stopping abruptly. Orville and Wilbur sat with their ears up, listening. As soon as the sound stopped, they howled in response and took off into the mine.

"Orville! Wilbur!" Arley yelled, but they kept going.

Muggs and Brute looked at each other and then took off, too, their short legs skattling along.

"Muggs! Brute!" she yelled, but they were gone, too.

Even though she knew what the sound was, and that the dogs were supposed to run into the mine, it still made the hair on the back of her neck stand up. And even though she knew the dogs would be safe—as safe as they could be inside an explosion-damaged firetrap—she still was awash with anxiety.

Morgan, in his black clothes, materialized out of the dark adit like a magic trick. "You should come inside," he said. "Mr. Lockwood could be along any time now."

She shook her head. "You know I can't."

"Purvis and Prairie Martin and Outdoor John and Archie and Duncan and Wing and the dogs are all in there and they're fine. Maybe it's time for you." His voice was so gentle and persuasive she felt as if she was being hypnotized.

"I'm afraid," she said meekly.

"I know all about being afraid. I spent most of my childhood being afraid. You have to keep going anyhow."

"But I don't have to go into a mine. It's not a requirement."

"Don't you want to see the stuff that's caused so much trouble? The stuff Lockwood believes you'll be sending to someone else?"

The truth was she would love to see the osblindium, and not just for herself. If only her papa could know what he'd almost had—if he'd known where to look for it, how to recognize it, and believed he really could have found it. She wavered. But then she remembered about the dark, and the closed-in spaces, and the bats. "No," she said. "You can bring me some."

"Then you better get out of sight. You don't want Mr. Lockwood to find you out here and wreck your plan." Morgan stood watching as she made her way back behind the rocks where Millicent and Anabelle waited. Then he turned and went back into the Never Mine.

Her sleepless night was catching up with her as

she leaned against Anabelle's warm side watching her graze on the little wet wildflowers between the rocks, and she almost fell asleep standing up. Just as she jerked herself awake, she heard the sound of hooves on stone, and voices. Male voices. She sneaked through the rocky jumble until she was close enough to hear what they were saying.

SIXTEEN

"IT WOULD HAVE SAVED us a lot of trouble if Morgan had started looking here first instead of last," Arley heard Mr. Lockwood say.

He came into sight on one of the spavined nags from Mickey's livery stable. The poor creature was poking along, resentful at having his nice nap interrupted for an actual customer.

Charles Randall followed on an equally rickety plug. "I believe he was concentrating on the mines you had already purchased."

"Completely wrong-headed," Mr. Lockwood said, waving his hand. "A mere technicality. Sooner or later

I'll own them all, now that I know the stuff is really here. Little Miss Pickett can't hold out forever. Even without Archie, that traitor, I've got the means to make her cooperate."

Not for long, Arley thought pugnaciously. *And I may be little but I'm tougher than you think.*

"Have you got lamps, or candles, or something? I'll want to get a good look at this stuff. I've never seen it in the wild. And we need to stop our little trouble-maker before she hacks it up too much."

"All set," Randall said.

They left their horses in the clearing and, as they entered the mine, Arley heard Mr. Lockwood say, "What's this?"

"Looks like a note," Charles Randall said. "What's it say?"

"It says, deth to introoders. Whoever wrote this is a very bad speller. And what's with all these little pictures—Indians with bows and arrows, and toma-hawks and spears? Is this meant to scare us off?" He laughed as if he had just been told a hilarious joke.

"I told you what Miss Bernaise said about the In-dian spirits who guard these mountains," Charles Ran-dall said in a tense tone. "Could that be from them?"

"I wasn't aware spirits had a written language,"

Mr. Lockwood said scornfully. "And even if they do, I don't think this is it. Besides, I'm not an easy man to scare, as you know."

"Wait. Here's another note, on this rock," Charles Randall said. "It says—oh, I see what you mean about the spelling—it says, No trespasin. Privat propitee. And it has the same little pictures around the edges. Somebody doesn't want us here."

"Of course they don't. Has that ever discouraged me before?" Mr. Lockwood said. "Whoever, or whatever, is leaving these messages, they're going to have to do better than that to make me think twice. Come on, let's get in there."

Their voices got fainter as they went into the mine, then suddenly echoed enough for Arley to hear Charles Randall say, "Those notes are all over the place," and Mr. Lockwood say, "Ignore them. Hey, look at this. Somebody's put these little candles around. That's a big help."

"But why would somebody do that?" Charles Randall asked.

"Who cares? It helps us see our way."

Then the voices faded completely away as they went deeper inside.

This is all going wrong, Arley thought. They were supposed to be scared by the threatening notes, and by Prairie Martin's gnome candles. Everdene had said

Sidney Lockwood wasn't superstitious, but to Arley's way of thinking, anything funny that happened in a mine should be enough to scare you out of it. Her plan had already gone so wrong, she was sure the rest of it would be a bust, too. And all her boarders, and Wing and Duncan and the dogs, too, were in there, not suspecting their efforts would not only be unsuccessful, but would be laughed at.

She rambled around the clearing fretting for a while before she got an idea. Taking her little knife from her pocket, and spilling a few dog biscuits with it, she sawed halfway through the saddle cinches on Charles Randall's and Mr. Lockwood's horses. Then she rambled some more, wringing her hands like a damsel in distress in a Penny Dreadful. When she realized what she was doing, she stopped it at once. Those dim damsels were always waiting for somebody to show up and rescue them. In her real life experience, you had to be ready to do your own rescuing.

The trouble was, she thought she'd figured out a way to do that, and now it was going all haywire.

At that moment Bridget and Everdene arrived on borrowed mules.

"Did they come?" Everdene asked, dismounting.

"They're inside. Looking for me so they can stop me from taking samples."

"Mr. Lockwood made Charles Randall cut the telegraph wires before they left town," Bridget said. "George the Hermit saw him do it. Mr. Lockwood didn't waste any time making sure you couldn't contact his competitors about your osblindium. Not that you were really going to do it."

"He sure thinks of everything. And nothing's going the way it's supposed to. They found the notes, but you're right, Mr. Lockwood isn't superstitious at all. And he wasn't afraid. Prairie Martin's candles didn't do it either. Charles Randall might have been a little nervous, but Mr. Lockwood didn't even slow down. I don't think this is going to work. And now I'm worried about everybody in there."

"Sidney's hard to discourage, that's for sure. Unless we're talking about marriage. Then it's easy. So we need to start thinking about Plan B."

"Everdene, at our meeting we went through the whole alphabet. This was the only plan we thought had any chance at all."

"My plan would have worked," Everdene said grimly.

"Well, we don't want to have to come visit you in prison while you're serving time for murder," Arley said, "so forget it."

Arley and Bridget took the mules behind the rocks.

"It's looking like an equine convention back here," Bridget said.

"I'm leaving Charles Randall's and Mr. Lockwood's horses where they are in front of the mine because I cut their saddle cinches. I wanted them to be able to leap on when they come running out, and then fall off halfway down the mountain. Only now I don't think they're going to come running out."

"Brilliant about the saddle cinches," Bridget said. "Let's wait on the running out part."

"I'm getting such a bad feeling about this," Arley said. "How could I not have seen how stupid my plan was?"

"Don't be so hard on yourself," Everdene said. "I knew Sidney wasn't superstitious, but it sounded wild enough even to me that I thought it could work."

She stood at the mine entrance, her pearl-handled derringer in her hand. "If it does work, how long do you think it'll take?" she asked.

"Shouldn't take very long," Arley said. "I didn't think it would take even this long."

After a couple more minutes of pacing the clearing, Everdene said, "I can't stand this. I'm going in. Maybe I can help. Maybe Archie needs some help." And she walked right into the mine and kept going.

"Archie?" Bridget and Arley said in unison. Then Arley said, "She's worried about Archie?"

And Bridget said, "When did she get so worried about Archie?" After a pause, she added, "Maybe she has a point. Duncan is in there, too." And she also walked straight into the mine and kept going.

Everybody I know is in there, Arley thought. *Even all my dogs.* She was already thinking of Muggs and Brute as hers. She would never let them go back to Charles Randall or Sidney Lockwood. If something happened to any of them she would be all alone, with only Mickey and Clarence and George the Hermit and a few ratty miners for company.

That prospect took her to the mine entrance. Sometimes a bigger fear can overcome a smaller one. All she could see in the gloom were the crumpled notes Mr. Lockwood had tossed to the ground. She took a few more steps, so that she was just inside the mine. From there she could see more of the notes lying, discarded, on the ground. All of Purvis's beautiful work, ignored. She bent to retrieve them. If the worst happened, at least she'd have them to remember him by.

The patter of rain began behind her, outside, as she followed the trail of notes, forgetting—or perhaps making herself forget—that it was taking her deeper into the mine. The flickers of light that Mr. Lockwood had been unimpressed with helped guide her. The little gnomes stuck into the rocks above and around her, their heads issuing tiny flames, seemed plenty eerie to her. And the dim firelight illuminated the many pairs of shining eyes glowing in the darkness. Even though Arley knew what she was seeing, her heart thumped so hard it hurt, and in spite of the warm air in the mine, she couldn't stop shivering. But apparently Mr. Lockwood had dismissed the eyes, too.

Notwithstanding the thumping and the shivering, she wasn't as terrified of the mine as she'd thought she'd be. Maybe, she considered, it was because she was surrounded by evidence of her friends, and because there were bigger things to be terrified of. When she spotted the birthday marmot from her bedroom perched on an upside-down bucket, she almost laughed out loud. Behind him was one of Outdoor John's less successful efforts—a stuffed prairie dog whose eyes were slightly crossed. But in the dark, by wavering light, if you didn't know what you were seeing, it could have been any kind of vicious little animal, ready to spring. At least it could have seemed that way to Arley.

The glass eyes followed her, peering from every irregularity in the rock, glittering malevolently. As she went farther in, her footsteps got smaller and smaller until she was barely moving. Only then did she notice how smooth the path was. From what she'd been told by her boarders, who had looked into the Never Mine after the explosion, the passageways had been clogged with rock and debris. Now, someone had very patiently cleared the way while he looked for what he had been sure was there. She felt a new little pang of possessive affection for the Never Mine. And something similar for Morgan.

As she stood in the flickering light, she heard strains of eerie music overlain by blood-curdling howls and yips, exaggerated by the echoing qualities of the twisting tunnels. Then shouts began ringing out: "Go!" and "You are cursed!" and "Beware!"

The din got louder and louder as the voices overlapped with the music and the howling and the echoes until nothing was intelligible—it was all just clashing noise. Then Arley heard two shots penetrate the pandemonium, followed by total dead silence.

Arley put her hand to her mouth. Had Everdene finally plugged not just Mr. Lockwood, but Charles Randall, too? She was horrified. And indignant. Nothing like that was supposed to happen in *her* plan. Or in her mine. That would *really* make the spirits mad.

"I warned you," she heard Everdene shout.

"There are penalties for what you just did," Mr. Lockwood answered.

Arley breathed again. He was still alive! And un-harmed, she gathered from the strength of his voice. She had the odd sensation of being relieved and disap-pointed at the same time.

"There are penalties for trespassing," Morgan said, "which is what you're doing."

"I'd like to see you do something about it," Mr. Lockwood said. "If your idea of intimidation is dogs, harmonicas, and stuffed animals, I can see I don't have anything to worry about."

"You're forgetting about me," Archie growled.

"Surprisingly easy to do," Mr. Lockwood sneered. "You don't dare harm me. My office knows where I am. If anything happens to me, there'd be investigators all over the place. You couldn't run far enough to hide from them. And, as you know, I don't always depend on traditional law enforcement methods."

Silence followed. Big, defeated silence.

Then Arley could hear, faintly in the background, Purvis saying, "What?" and Prairie Martin saying, "Shhh!" and Outdoor John whimpering.

Then Mr. Lockwood laughed. "And I can see my os-blindium there in the walls where it looks like there was an explosion. That *is* osblindium, right, Morgan?"

"Whatever it is, it isn't yours," Morgan said.

"It soon will be," he said. "I always get my way."

"He always does," Charles Randall confirmed.

"How?" Purvis asked.

"Shhh!" Prairie Martin said.

And Outdoor John kept whimpering.

"Spirits not liking this kind of talk," Wing said.

"Spirits!" Mr. Lockwood said. "Bunch of hogwash."

"No," Wing said. "They live up here. They watch."

"Then let them watch me make a fortune—another one—on osblindium. Come on, Randall. Miss Pickett doesn't seem to be around, so let's get out of here."

Tears of furious impotence welled in Arley's eyes. She hadn't been able to see anybody, but she'd heard every word. Their plan had failed and now they were all vulnerable to whatever nefarious schemes Mr. Lockwood chose to use on them.

She heard footsteps coming toward her, and Mr. Lockwood's voice, becoming louder, saying, "Did you see all that osblindium? There was enough just where we were standing to buy this whole town ten times over. I don't care what that Pickett girl thinks she's going to do. I'm going to get this mine."

Arley stepped into a fissure in the tunnel wall partially blocked by a tumble of rock debris. As Mr. Lockwood and Charles Randall came closer, her indignation and wrath overwhelmed her and involuntarily she hissed, "Sidney Lockwood!" The sound echoed and ric-ocheted impressively through the tunnel.

"What?" she heard him say.

"I didn't say anything," Charles Randall said.

"Yes, you did. You said my name." Evidently they had stopped walking just outside her hiding place.

"No, I didn't. Why would I do that?"

"I have no idea. But you did it. And don't argue with me."

"Sidney Lockwood," she hissed again, this time on purpose.

"There. You did it again," he said.

"You were standing right there in front of me," Charles Randall said. "Did you see my lips move?"

"How could I? The light's not so good in here. Now stop it."

"Charles Randall," Arley said in a hoarse whisper.

"Now you're saying your own name?" Mr. Lockwood said. "What's the matter with you?"

"Put your hand over my mouth," Charles Randall said, "and see what happens."

Mr. Lockwood must have done that because Arley heard him say, "Try and say something now," followed by muffled sounds.

"Charles Randall. You who served time for fraud.

You must leave this mountain," Arley rasped. Why not? It was worth a try. For good measure she tossed a rock up at the tunnel ceiling and it produced a satisfying shower of gravel.

"Huh?" Mr. Lockwood said. "Did you do that, Randall?"

More muffled grunts came from Charles Randall; then a gasp and, "How could I? You were gagging me. And why would I bring up that old...you know."

"What's going on here?" Mr. Lockwood asked.

"Maybe...maybe it's those spirits," Charles Randall said with a tremor in his voice. "The ones you don't believe in. Maybe they believe in you. And me, too."

"I *am* well-known, that's true. But I don't think my reputation has spread as far as the astral realm. Somebody's trying to play another trick on us."

Arley gulped, and then straightened her spine. Mr. Lockwood was willing to do anything to stop her from selling her mine to someone else. She was willing to do anything—well, *almost* anything—to get him out of Grubstake.

"This is no trick," she intoned. "Your heart is unclean. Your motives are foul. You must leave this mountain."

"Don't be ridiculous," Mr. Lockwood said indignantly. "I don't care *who* you are. There's a king's ransom waiting for me in here. This mine is meant to be mine."

Arley couldn't decide whether to be amused or disgusted at Mr. Lockwood, arguing even with an unseen speaker.

"It is not for you," Arley told him sternly.

"Who else could it be for, then?" he asked. "I'm the biggest tycoon there is. I deserve it."

"Do not question!" she thundered, losing patience and throwing another rock, releasing more pebbles.

"Hey!" Mr. Lockwood exclaimed. "Cut that out! You're not scaring me."

"Um, Mr. Lockwood," Charles Randall said. "Maybe we should be listening."

"I *am* listening," he said. "What do you think I'm doing?"

"I mean, maybe we should go. It sounds angry."

"Don't be silly. It's just one of those old miners. What can he do except annoy me?"

"Cave in the tunnel on us?" Charles Randall suggested.

Arley threw another rock for emphasis.

"Hmmm," Mr. Lockwood said, unimpressed. "If that's the best he can do..."

At that moment there was a bolt of lightning so incandescent that it lit the tunnel for an instant with blazing light, followed immediately by a blast of thunder that shook the ground they stood on. Arley saw bright spots before her eyes as two more concussions of thunder jolted them. Rocks rained from the ceiling and Arley shrank back against the wall.

She should have been terrified, and part of her was. But the rest of her was exhilarated at the way the weather, and maybe the real spirits, were cooperating, and she took advantage of it.

"Do you want more?" she snarled. "Do you want me to bury you?"

"No," Charles Randall squealed, and she heard his footsteps running away.

"Do you, Sidney Lockwood?" she asked.

"As if you could," he said. "And even if you could, you wouldn't take a chance on burying all that osblindium."

Another explosion of lightning and thunder shook the mine.

"I'll bury it in a second to keep it from you," Arley said, meaning it. "I've got dynamite and I'm not afraid to use it. It'll cost you a fortune to dig that osblindium out again. And I'll come back and blow it up every time you uncover it. It'll cost you every penny you have and I'll make sure you never take an ounce of osblindium out of the Never Mine."

Another huge clap of thunder shook the mine.

"Every penny?" Mr. Lockwood digested that thought. "You'd really blow it up?"

"Without a second thought."

There was a long silence. "Really? You'd blow it up?" he asked again.

"Yep."

More silence. Then he said, "You're even stupider than I thought. But I believe you. I'll just have to find another mountain. There'll be more osblindium. There's always more. Whoever said less is more has got it all wrong. The only thing that's more is *more*."

"Go!" Arley spoke. "Now! Before you regret it."

"I already regret it," he muttered sourly, but she heard his footsteps leaving.

Climbing out of the rock fissure, Arley followed him stealthily through the tunnel. In the watery light from the entrance, she could see Mr. Lockwood pushing a staggering Charles Randall aside so hard he fell down. Mr. Lockwood stepped over him and kept going, out into the downpour. Charles Randall crawled after him crying, "Don't leave me! Don't leave me!"

Mr. Lockwood didn't even pause.

Arley had to try very hard not to feel sorry for Charles Randall. In spite of the fact that he was a crook, a liar, an ex-con, and an arrogant knucklehead, she took no pleasure in watching him crawl through the mud. From her boarders she had learned that even the crustiest exterior could hide a fearful little boy.

She made herself stay where she was as he got to his feet and took off again. By the time she reached the entrance of the Never Mine, Mr. Lockwood had mounted up and gone—at least for a ways, Arley thought—and Charles Randall was struggling to get his feet into the dripping and slippery stirrups of his mount. Finally he managed, kicked the poor old plug in the ribs—which made Arley angry at him all over again—and took off through sheets of rain.

Still standing in the shadows, Arley wiggled her fingers at him and whispered, "Bye-bye." Then her knees gave out under her and she collapsed onto a rock. She was still sitting there when the others came hesitantly along the tunnel.

SEVENTEEN

"ARE YOU ALL RIGHT?" Morgan asked. And as soon as she nodded that she was, he asked, "Are they gone?"

"Yes. But they may be walking part of the way. I cut their saddle cinches."

Morgan laughed—the first nice laugh she'd heard from him—and put his arm around her and squeezed. "That's my girl," he said.

What? Arley thought. *Who?*

Then the others all were talking at once.

"Arley, Arley, did you hear that voice? What was that?"

"I burned up all my gnomes and they didn't scare him at all. My harmonica either. He didn't even shiver."

"I hope I can find all my eyeballs again. That was the scariest thunder and lightning I ever heard."

"Don't worry, the rest of us all shiver when you play."

"Man, I'm glad I don't work for him no more."

"See, Archie? Doesn't doing the right thing make you feel better than criminal activities?"

"I'm going to write an article about what he wanted to do here and put it out on the telegraph for other newspapers to pick up so he can never try this in any other town."

"Oooh, Duncan, that's so heroic."

"Out of the mud grows the lotus."

"What really happened?"

"Who was talking?"

"Who made that thunder and lightning?"

There was a lot of barking as all four dogs got over their shock and cut loose.

Then everybody shut up while Arley told the whole story. "Mr. Lockwood might not believe in ghosts, and I'm not one hundred percent sure I do, but that storm couldn't have come up at a better time," she finished.

"We must thank the mountain spirits for that," Wing said. "In case they were responsible."

"No kidding," Arley said. "All together now. One, two, three."

Everybody yelled, "Thank you! Thank you!" And then they burst into gales of hysterical, relieved laughter.

—◦◦◦◦◦—

Little by little, the storm moved on over the mountains, the lightning and thunder diminishing into distant rumbles, the deluge moderating into the ordinary rain they were used to.

Arley asked, "Can we really believe they're gone for good?"

"Let's go see," Morgan said.

It was quite a parade of mules being led down the soggy, slippery mountain by Morgan on his magnificent Millicent and accompanied by four filthy dogs. As they rode up the main street of Grubstake, Clarence came out of the mercantile, and George the Hermit stood in the door of the livery with Mickey to watch them.

In front of the Spittoon, Charles Randall sat, sopping wet, at the reins of the livery's crummy carriage. The carriage door that wouldn't stay shut revealed Mr. Lockwood and Lacey Bernaise, with Fifi in her lap, along with Dr. and Mrs. Bernaise and some luggage.

"Whip that horse!" Mr. Lockwood shouted. "Get to my train! I've wasted enough time in this armpit of a place."

Charles Randall flapped the reins and the horse took off at his usual leisurely pace.

"Whip him!" Mr. Lockwood screeched. But Charles Randall didn't. He didn't want one bit more trouble with those old Indians. The carriage lumbered away.

"I can see the bullet hole I put in his hat from here," Everdene said with satisfaction. "And that's exactly where I meant it to be, Arley, so don't give me that look. The other one went into the wall, didn't it, not into him. Now, everybody into the Spittoon. We're drying off and then we're celebrating."

"I have fresh donuts," Wing said. "I will bring."

"He never even asked about Muggs or Brute," Arley said to Morgan. "He just left them."

"What did you expect?"

—◦◦⊙◦⊙◦◦—

Soon everyone, including Mickey, George the Hermit, Clarence, and the other leftover residents of Grubstake, was in the Spittoon. Prairie Martin was showing off with his harmonica, playing barely recognizable tunes until no one could tolerate the music or the accompaniment of four howling dogs. Everdene served up beer and sarsaparilla and peanuts in the shell, and Wing donated dozens of scrumptious fresh donuts. Morgan had five.

As the story got told to the other Grubs, Bridget

went upstairs to see if Charles Randall had left anything interesting behind. She came back down with a pile of papers she laid out on the bar.

"What's that?" Everdene asked.

"Deeds," Bridget said. "The deeds for all the mines Lockwood bought. And they're all marked 'Void And Cancelled.' He's giving them back. He must really believe all the osblindium is in the Never Mine. And he just wants to wash his hands of Grubstake."

"But what about the miners who sold out and left?" Arley asked.

"I guess they still own their mines. Of course, most of them will never know that since we don't know how to reach them to tell them."

"Then we need to keep those deeds in a safe place," Everdene said. "Just in case. Once Duncan gets his article out, we might get some of them back."

Morgan sat down next to Arley. "I'd like to show you your osblindium before I go," he said. "I promise you've never seen anything like it."

"I believe you," she said. "But I don't know if I can go in there again."

"The first time's the hardest. You've done that."

"But then I was so scared and mad I hardly noticed. Besides, all my friends were in there. I wanted to be with them."

After a moment of silence he said, "Yes. Friends are important. And so is your osblindium. Won't you let me show it to you?"

She hesitated. "Can't you bring me out a piece?"

"It's so much more amazing to see it in its natural place. I'll be leaving soon. Can you do it as a good-bye present for me?" When she didn't answer, he said, "I *did* help get rid of Lockwood. And I did find osblindium in your mine. It's going to make you very rich."

"How many zeroes?" Arley asked.

Morgan laughed again.

"You look so different when you laugh," she said. "Younger."

"Do I? I'm not much of a laugher."

"I noticed. You should try it more."

"If I promise to try, will you let me show you the osblindium?" he asked quietly.

How could she say no to that? "But if I need to leave, you won't try to make me stay in there, right?"

"Right." He stood up.

"You mean *now*?" she squeaked.

Morgan took Arley's hand and pulled her to her feet. "I don't know how much longer I'll be here. We might not have another chance."

"But, the party—"

"It'll be going on for days. You won't miss anything."

"But—"

"Come on." He pulled her to the door and out to the hitching post where Millicent and Anabelle waited. Anabelle made it clear she wasn't thrilled about going up the mountain again, balking and sulking—which was about the way Arley felt, too. But they were both going anyway.

Once they reached the Never Mine, Morgan dismounted and helped Arley down from Anabelle. "Don't be afraid," he said. "Any spirits in there will be glad it's you."

"They will?"

"Nobody deserves their osblindium more than you do. Your father died here—"

"It was his own darn fault," she said, interrupting.

Morgan shrugged and continued, "—you refused to sell out to Mr. Lockwood, you single-handedly drove away a very bad man. A couple of very bad men, one of whom seems to have taken on a woman who will give him just what he deserves—"

"You mean Charles Randall and Lacey?" she asked, interrupting again.

He nodded and went on, "—and you did everything you could to protect the other miners from being taken advantage of. I think those spirits should want to give you a medal."

"Well, if they do, I'll take it," she said.

Morgan laughed, lit a candle, took her hand, and drew her into the mine. He had to tug some to keep her moving. Before she knew it, they were so deeply inside that the feeble light from the candle seemed ridiculously anemic. She was way too conscious of the tons of rock over her head, and the knowledge that she couldn't go back now, alone and in the dark, no matter how much she wanted to.

After a while Morgan stopped. He set his candle down on an upturned bucket, pulled other candles from his boots, lit them, and added them to the bottom of the bucket. "Look," he said, pointing to the wall.

There seemed to be a dark rainbow twining through the rock. The colors were deep indigo and grape, ruby and cobalt, and they seemed alive. The band of colors shimmered and glowed in the candle-light as if it had breath, beautiful and unearthly.

"That's osblindium?" Arley whispered.

"That's the stuff."

"How come my papa couldn't see this?"

"His explosion must have exposed it. It was buried until then."

"So his last act, stupid as it was, left this for me?" She gazed for a while and then said, "Sidney Lockwood doesn't deserve even one little piece of that."

"Right. And look. It's all over the place."

He knew his rocks, all right. The dark rainbow ran under their feet, and over their heads, and on both sides of the tunnel.

"It's in the rubble from the explosion, too," Morgan said. "I saved that for you. You can sell that to get the money to start the commercial mining operation."

"You thought of everything."

"Walk along a little ways with me. You'll see it goes on and on. Probably into some of the other mines." He took up a candle and led her along the tunnel.

As Arley looked at all the osblindium she forgot she was even inside a mine. More like being inside a prism. Or a kaleidoscope.

"Did you know the miners call it pay dirt?" she asked Morgan.

"Yes. But I'd never call anything this magnificent *dirt*."

"All this makes me feel sort of faint," she said. "But thank you for making me come in here. I don't know if I'll want to do it a lot, but I'm glad I did it now."

"I knew you would be. That's why I pushed. I wanted to make sure you saw it before I left."

"There's not exactly a big demand for my rooms, so there's no hurry."

"There is for me. I need a job. A paying job. I have

my obligations, and employment opportunities aren't so plentiful here."

"I'm going to need a manager for my mining operation," Arley said, gesturing at the shimmering tunnel walls. "I don't know how long before there'll be a paycheck, but eventually there will be one. And I think you're qualified. If you're interested, that is."

Morgan let out a long breath. "There's nothing I'd rather do."

"Okay, then." She stuck out her hand. "Now I'm not just your landlady, I'm your boss, too. You okay with working for a girl?"

"I'm okay with working for *this* girl." He shook her hand and then held on to it. The candle he held in his other hand cast a warm, wavering radiance around them.

"I need to sit down for a minute," Arley said, dropping onto a pile of rocks filled with osblindium. "I've had a very big day. Oh. I feel like I'm sitting on a pile of money."

Morgan laughed. She had to admit she liked seeing that, how his dark eyes crinkled up and his stern face softened. And she liked being the one who could make that happen.

—◦◦◉◦◦◉◦◦—

Outside, the sun was setting and the rain had begun again. Inside, the party was going strong. Bridget was sitting on Duncan's lap; Purvis, Prairie Martin, and Outdoor John were throwing peanuts in the air and catching them in their mouths (though Purvis kept forgetting to take the shells off); Everdene and Archie had their heads together over something at the bar; and the other miners had their arms around each other, singing their heads off.

Although Arley tried to enter into the festivities, her brain was feeling too muddled and messy to be seen in public. "I'm going home to bed," she told Morgan.

"It's raining. You'll get wet," Morgan said. "Let me walk with you."

She held up her hand, palm out. "Keep partying. I've been wet before. It's temporary." She headed out the door and went off down the wooden sidewalk. Her own company was already too complicated. There wasn't room for anybody else's.

EIGHTEEN

THINGS WEREN'T MUCH BETTER the next morning. Arley had hardly slept—and not just because the dogs and the boarders made such a racket when they'd finally come in. All of them were still asleep when she went out, leaving a pot of porridge on the stove, and bread and butter waiting on the table.

At the Spittoon, Everdene and Archie were still— or again—deep in conversation, now at a table, ignoring the party mess around them. Bridget was washing glasses and Mickey, as usual, was asleep on the floor. His hat had fallen off, and Arley could see the patchy haircut. She couldn't say he looked any worse than he usually did.

"You left early last night," Bridget said. "Anything wrong?"

"I went to look at my osblindium. And then...then I had to go to bed." Arley picked up a towel and began drying glasses.

"Pretty intense, huh?" Bridget said sympathetically.

"You don't know the half of it."

The door burst open and Duncan came in, waving a piece of paper, his face white.

"What is it, Petkins?" Bridget asked, startled.

Petkins? Arley thought.

"You won't believe this," Duncan said, laying the paper on the bar. It was a telegram. "Last night after George the Hermit spliced the telegraph line, I wrote up what had happened here and sent it out to the biggest newspapers in the country. And this morning I got this." He pushed the telegram toward Bridget. "Read it."

"Dear Duncan," she read. "I was in the newspaper office in Denver last night when your wire story came through. Stop. I was so proud. Stop. I knew you could do it. Stop. The night I left I decided you needed to be free of me to come into yourself. Stop. And I was right. Stop. I also knew Everdene was never going to give me the time of day. Stop. Forgive me for scaring you. Stop. I hope you understand. Stop. Any time you want a newspaper job in Denver, come see me. Stop. I'm managing

editor. Stop. You are a credit to the profession of journalism. Stop. Love, your father. Stop." Bridget looked
up at him. "Your father's alive, Petkins?"

"What's with all those 'stop's?" Arley asked.

"That's how you make a period on the telegraph,"
Duncan said absently. Turning back to Bridget, he
said, "Apparently. He must have waited out the blizzard alone in the train station and gotten on the next
train out. Or maybe he walked down the mountain in
the blizzard. He always thought he could do anything
he put his mind to—maybe he was right."

"Are you going to Denver?" Bridget asked.

"Certainly not. I think Grubstake's going to need a
newspaper more than ever soon. And I really don't
want to work for my father."

"Good," she said. "I'm glad."

"I'm glad, too," he said, gazing at her adoringly.

Arley could have been on fire and they wouldn't
have noticed. She went to the table where Everdene
and Archie were still deep in talk.

"Did you hear that?" she asked.

"What?" Everdene said, looking up.

"Sebastian McKenzie is alive. He works for a newspaper in Denver. He's proud of Duncan. So he's no
longer a blot on the family escutcheon."

"That's so nice," Everdene said distractedly. "I knew he'd come around eventually."

She was turning back to Archie when Arley said, "What's going on here?"

"Oh. You won't believe how much Archie and I have in common. Besides a revulsion for Sidney Lockwood. We're both hard workers. We're both responsible people. We both have high standards for ourselves. We both"— she turned to gaze fondly at Archie—"have survived early disappointments in love." He returned her gaze, looking as if he'd fallen out of a very tall tree and was amazed to find himself unhurt.

Arley remembered Everdene telling her once that people in love had brains that didn't work. But she thought Everdene was wrong. Their brains *did* work. They worked in a positive, warmhearted, sweet-tempered way that was better than when they weren't in love. Love was a changing thing, but changing in the right direction. It was love gone wrong that made people cranky and sad and bad-tempered. Maybe Everdene was in the process of discovering that.

Arley felt about as necessary as Mickey at that moment. No one even noticed when she went out the door.

At the bakery, Wing looked up from kneading dough when she came in. "Morning, Arley," he said.

"Hi, Wing. What's cooking?"

"Bread is, as usual. But today I make something new, too. Look." He handed her a folded cookie. "Open."

She cracked it open and a little slip of paper fell out. Arley read, "*Always do the right thing. Even when you don't want to.* What's this?" she asked.

"What you said I needed. Way to make people pay for my advice. I put it inside cookie."

"Wing, that's brilliant." She popped the cookie into her mouth. "And the cookie's good, too," she said with her mouth full. "What are you calling them?"

"Haven't decided yet. Advice Cookies sound like lecture. Wise Cookies too pretentious. Surprise Cookies sound like might blow up. I keep thinking." He gave her a long look and said, "You left party early yesterday. How come?"

"Morgan took me to see the osblindium in the Never Mine. It was serious. Kind of overwhelmed me."

"How about Mr. Morgan? He overwhelm you, too?"

Arley blinked. "What do you mean?"

"Morgan. He change his whole life since he came here. Must be reason."

"The reason is he hated working for Mr. Lockwood."

"He always hated working for Mr. Lockwood. Why *now* he change?"

"If there's something you want me to know, Wing, you better just tell me because I can't crack your inscrutable code."

"He find something he like much better than Mr. Lockwood. Something he *want* more than he want to work for Mr. Lockwood. That *you,* Arley. Well? How you like my code now?"

"I...but I'm not the kind of person somebody would feel like that about. I'm not like Everdene. Or even Lacey."

"Maybe being like *you* is enough. For Mr. Morgan, anyway. You want to take some cookies home?"

Arley nodded. But she wasn't ready for home yet. Going from being practically penniless to being the owner of maybe the wealthiest mine in the West was a pretty colossal adjustment. Going from somebody reading Penny Dreadfuls to being somebody starring in one was even bigger.

"So, how you feel about Mr. Morgan?" Wing asked, sliding a tray of cookies from the oven.

"Don't talk to me. I have too much to think about right now," Arley said.

They were silent through four more batches of cookies. As Wing took the last tray from the oven, Arley said, "Okay. Give me two dozen. I'm going home."

As she walked, she felt the sun on her back. She looked up to see the mists among the mountains evaporating, and down to see a couple of determined daffodils unfurling from the mud.

Good, she thought. *Everdene can finally hang her swinging doors.*

Once home, she stood on the porch taking a lot of deep breaths. She was still breathing hard when the door opened and the four dogs came dashing out, yapping happily and tumbling over each other as they raced off down the sunny street. Morgan stood in the open doorway looking clean and rested and important all in black.

She'd taken so many deep breaths she'd made herself light-headed, and was seeing little stars in front of her eyes so that Morgan looked spangled and even more unreal than usual.

"Good morning, Arley," he said solemnly.

"Good morning. Are the others up? I've got cookies." She held out the sack from Wing's.

"They're still asleep. They had a big night last night. But I could eat a cookie."

"Okay," she said, pulling the sack closer to her. "But first I need to ask you some questions."

"Don't you want to come in?"

"No. I'm afraid I won't do it if I wait."

"Sounds serious."

"It is." She took a few more deep breaths, until she got dizzy enough to go on. "What if we brought the orphans here? We could turn the Opera House into an orphanage."

For a moment Morgan looked as light-headed as Arley felt. Then he said, "But why?"

"Don't you think we need some younger Grubs around here? And it would give all the dogs someone to play with. Might keep them out of so much trouble. And you could keep an eye on your investment."

"All right," he said. "That's an excellent idea. Any more questions?"

She nodded. "Why do you wear black all the time? Even your handkerchiefs are black."

"I'm color-blind. Nothing to do with fashion—it's just easier. More?"

She nodded again. "Why do you carry skeleton keys?"

"I like being able to keep my things locked up and private. I never could in the orphanage. It's satisfying." He looked closely at her. "Why all the questions?"

"Just trying to get to know my...my mine manager better. You know, I think I do have to go sit down." She brushed past him into the parlor and plopped down on the settee, the sack of cookies on her lap.

Morgan followed her and knelt at her feet. "Arley, will you—" he began, just as Purvis, Prairie Martin, and Outdoor John came pounding down the stairs.

"Arley!" Prairie Martin said. "What's in the sack?"

"Arley!" Outdoor John said. "That was the best party I ever went to. And there wasn't anything to be afraid of. What's for breakfast?"

"Arley!" Purvis said. "Why is Morgan on the floor?"

Morgan jumped to his feet, startled.

Arley stood, too. "Morgan was on the floor because... well, we'll have to talk about that later. Right now we're having cookies for breakfast. And I'm making you all members of my board of directors for my mining operation. Maybe all the dogs should be, too, so they get some respect around here." She headed for the kitchen with everyone following her, asking questions.

"What's a board of directors?" Purvis asked.

"Do we have to decide things?" Prairie Martin asked.

"Does it pay?" Outdoor John asked.

But Arley wasn't listening to the questions. She was still talking. "We need to get organized because we have a mine to run—we'll have to get the train coming more often, won't we?—an orphanage to establish—we'll have to evict the marmots from the schoolhouse—a lending library to start—I'm never going to have time to read all those Penny Dreadfuls—at least one wedding to plan, maybe more—and a few trips to take. London first, I think."